aces♣up

aces ♣ up

LAUREN BARNHOLDT

DELACORTE PRESS

Copyright © 2010 by Lauren Barnholdt

All rights reserved. Published in the United States by Delacorte Press,
an imprint of Random House Children's Books,
a division of Random House, Inc., New York.

Delacorte Press is a registered trademark and the colophon is a trademark of
Random House, Inc.

Visit us on the Web! www.randomhouse.com/teens

Educators and librarians, for a variety of teaching tools, visit us at
www.randomhouse.com/teachers

Library of Congress Cataloging-in-Publication Data is available upon request.
ISBN 978-0-385-73874-3 (tr. pbk.)
ISBN 978-0-375-89583-8 (e-book)

The text of this book is set in 12-point Baskerville Book.

Book design by Angela Carlino

Printed in the United States of America

10 9 8 7 6 5 4 3 2 1

First Edition

To Kevin Cregg, for Turningstone,
Tully's, and everything else

acknowledgments

Thank you, thank you, thank you to:

My editors, Stephanie Elliott and Krista Vitola, for their wonderful guidance and advice

My agent, Alyssa Eisner Henkin, for being made of awesome

My sisters, Krissi and Kelsey, for being my best friends

Mandy Hubbard and Jessica Burkhart, for being fabulous e-mail buddies and always talking me down when I'm having writing-related freak-outs

My mom, for being there no matter what, always

My dad, for reading every single one of my books

Scott Neumyer, Jodi Yanarella, and the Gorvine family for their support

And last but not least, my amazing husband, Aaron, for making me the happiest I've ever been—I love you.

aces♣up

$\mathcal{I}$ will not freak out, I will not freak out, I will not freak out. It is only a *dress*. A flimsy, totally stretchable piece of fabric. A flimsy, totally stretchable piece of fabric that will not budge over my hips, but still. Not a big deal. In fact, I'm sure things like this happen all the time. I'll just march out of here, head into the office of my new boss, Adrienne, and calmly explain to her that the uniform they've given me just doesn't fit.

I mean, I indicated on my application that I'm a size

eight. And since they have somehow decided to give me a size *two* uniform, then really, they should be the ones apologizing to me. Isn't that some sort of sizeism? (Sizeism = like racism, only against people who aren't a size two or four.) They'll probably be so nervous I'm going to sue them for discrimination that I'll get some kind of bonus or something. You know, so that I'll keep my mouth shut.

I start to pull the dress off, but before I can get out of it, someone knocks on the door to the dressing room in the employee lounge, where I'm huddled with the dress stuck halfway up my hips.

"Who's in there?" a voice demands. A bossy, nasally, very *loud* voice. My boss, Adrienne.

"Um, it's me," I say. "Shannon." My voice comes out all strangled, and I clear my throat and try to sound normal. Maybe I just need someone to zip me up? Or I need to lie down on a bed somewhere, like I have to do when my jeans just come out of the dryer. Of course, there's no bed in here, they wouldn't put a *bed* in a dressing room, that would be a little ridiculous. And there's definitely not enough room to lie down on the floor, but maybe if I angled myself a little better, I could lean back and then—

"Who?"

"Shannon!" I say, louder this time. Maybe the uniform is vanity-sized, and so their two is actually a six. Like they do at the Gap. I give the dress a good yank, and it creeps up a little further over my hips. Hmmm.

I give it another tug, this time as hard as I can. Riiiiip. The sound of fabric tearing echoes through the dressing room as the side seam of the dress splits in two. Oops.

"What the hell was *that*?" More pounding. "There are customers waiting to be served!"

"Um, well," I say, throwing my sweatshirt over my head and opening the door to the stall. My face is burning with embarrassment, and I'm sure there are two big red splotches on my cheeks. "The thing is," I tell Adrienne, "I have a problem with my uniform. It doesn't fit." I hold up the shredded piece of fabric. "Or, um, it *didn't* fit." I give her a hopeful smile.

"You ripped it?" Adrienne asks, looking incredulous. She reaches out and fingers the material.

"Well, not on *purpose,* I would never do something like that on *purpose*." She looks at me blankly. "I thought it was vanity sized," I explain, still trying to stay positive.

"You tried to *shove* yourself into it, and you *split* it?"

"Well, not shove, exactly, it was more like . . . wedge." Adrienne is a few years older than me, and very, very scary. She has short black hair with thick bangs, and a dark red mouth. She wears lots of eyeliner and I'm pretty sure her boobs are fake. At my interview last week, when she asked me why I wanted this job, I told her I loved interacting with people, and she laughed, like she thought I was joking. I totally wasn't, but I did not want Adrienne to hate me and/or

3

think I was going to cause any kind of trouble, so I laughed, too.

If she finds out I'm only seventeen, I will be fired immediately. You have to be twenty-one to work as a cocktail waitress at the Collosio Casino, but I really, really need this job. My dad got fired from *his* job four months ago, and if I don't make my own money, there's no way I'll be able to go to Wellesley in the fall. And since I've already been accepted early admission, which means I'm not allowed to apply anywhere else, this is a bit of a problem. (I'm calling it a "bit of a problem" so that I don't freak myself out too much. The truth is it's a "bit of a problem" that has the potential to turn into a "really bad disaster." No money for Wellesley = no college.) So I bought a fake ID from this guy named Chris Harmon, who's in my fifth-period study hall, and here I am. Besides, I'll be twenty-one soon. Well. In, like, four years.

"It was too small," I say, holding the dress up in front of me, as if to demonstrate its too-small state. Adrienne's making me nervous, and the lights over-head are beating down on me. I brush my long brown hair out of my face and hope I don't start to sweat. "I am so, so sorry. I thought I marked down on my application that I'm a size eight, but apparently it ended up that—"

Adrienne sighs and rubs her temples, then looks at me like I'm a child she's babysitting. She sets her pen down on her clipboard. "What time is it, Shannon?"

Um, is this a trick question? "Five o'clock?" I try.

"Right. And what happens at five o'clock?"

"I start work?"

"Right. And if you come into work not ready to start working, *then* what happens at five o'clock?"

"Um, I don't start working?"

"Exactly."

"I'm sorry," I say again. "But I marked down on the application you gave me that I'm a size—"

Adrienne holds up a hand. "Look," she says, her blue eyes narrowing. She smells like some kind of violet perfume. "Can you hang or not? Because there are a lot of girls who would kill for this job." I'm not sure what "Can you hang?" means, but I have a feeling it's to be answered in the affirmative and does not involve having a uniform situation on day one. Also, I'm very wary now that she's said "There are a lot of girls who would kill for this job." That's what they kept telling Anne Hathaway's character in the movie *The Devil Wears Prada*. And things did not go so well for her.

"Yes," I say, squaring my shoulders and trying to look shocked, as if I can't believe she's asked such an insane question. I roll my eyes. "Of course. Of course I can hang." For ten dollars an hour plus tips, I can definitely hang. One hundred percent hanging.

"Then go get another uniform from the uniform closet," Adrienne says, pointing toward a door on the other side of the room. She snatches the ruined uniform out of my hands. "This one will have to come out

5

of your paycheck. And then get back here and we'll get you started on your training." She waves her hand and her black-tipped acrylic fingernails, dismissing me.

Fifteen minutes later, I'm in my new uniform (fits, but makes me look like a sausage—stretchy black fabric, a gathered waist, and a built-in bra that pushes your boobs together is not a good look for anyone), standing in the bar area with Mackenzie.

Mackenzie is the waitress who's training me. She looks like a Miss Hawaiian Tropic and *definitely* does not have a problem zipping up her uniform.

"Basically the tips are all you want to worry about," she's saying. "You want to take as many drink orders as possible, and get the drinks out as fast as possible."

She flips her long blond hair over her shoulder. I'm shadowing her, which, as far as I can tell, basically means I'm going to follow her around the casino all night, watching what she does. For this, I will earn my ten dollars an hour, with no tips.

But whatevs. I'm all about the big picture. Once I get the hang of it, I'll be out on my own, and then I'm sure I'll be making tons.

"Right," I say. I work on practicing what I learned from *The Secret,* that book that says whatever you think will actually become your reality, and conjure up an image of myself at Wellesley, walking on campus with a bag full of newly purchased schoolbooks in one hand and a grande peppermint latte in the other. Feeling cheered by my mental picture, I pull a tiny gray notebook out of my pocket and write, "as many drinks as possible, make them come out fast."

"What are you doing?" Mackenzie asks. She's wearing glitter eye shadow, and some of it has fallen onto her cheeks, giving her a sparkly glow.

"I'm writing down what you just said."

"You can't remember to serve as many drinks as possible?" She looks as if I've just said that I can't remember what my name is, or that I'm supposed to eat.

"Well, I probably would, *technically,* be able to remember it," I say. Which is true. I have a very good memory. "But if I write it down, then I'll definitely be *sure.*"

She looks at me blankly, and then I get it. Mackenzie is one of those girls who never, ever write things down. She probably shows up to her classes without notebooks or pens and is that annoying person who's always borrowing loose-leaf paper from everyone.

"What's that?" she asks, peering down at my notebook.

She's looking at the opposite page, where I've done a thorough calculation of my financial situation and how much I will need for Wellesley.

It's all broken down into subsets, like type of financial aid, type of cost, academic year. Then there's an overview at the bottom.

For example, my freshman year overview looks like this:

Total cost of tuition, room, and board =
    $48,786
Total loans = $3,245
Grants = $18,141
Total amount of financial aid = $21,386
Total amount needed = $27,400

"Oh, that," I say. "That's just a breakdown of how much money I need to pay my tuition." Then I realize I'm already supposed to be in college, so I rush on. "For all my other years at school." She's looking at me blankly again, so I show her the page. "See? For example, I need twenty thousand dollars still to pay my tuition. Now, they have payment plans, but if you don't pay, then they can totally hold your transcripts and your credits." I bite my lip. "At least, I think they can. I heard it from one of my sister's friends. Her mom lost her job and then her loans got—"

"Whatever," Mackenzie says, putting her hands up like I need to stop talking.

Suddenly, I am suspicious of her. Anyone who can look this good in the Collosio Casino waitressing uniform and is also questioning the validity of taking copious notes and making diagrams and flowcharts cannot be trusted. That size double-zero I saw in the uniform closet? Definitely hers.

"Grab that tray," she instructs, pointing to an empty one in the kitchen near the bar. Great. Now she's bossy. I pick it up and watch as she starts loading my tray with the already-filled little plastic cups sitting on the bar. "These," she says, "are what you fill your tray with. Water, soda, beer. They're the most common drinks people want. But you need to keep a pad with you in case you need to take special orders."

Right. I write down, "Fill tray with H_2O, soda, beer. Keep notebook for special orders."

"Look, stop writing crap down," Mackenzie says. The lights overhead bounce off her perfectly white, perfectly straight teeth. "We don't have time. Keep filling your tray."

I do what she says, and when I'm finished, the tray weighs about three thousand pounds. I am then expected to heft it over my head and follow Mackenzie through the bar and into the poker room. Immediately I feel like maybe I've pulled a muscle. Mackenzie hoists her tray over her head like it's a feather and starts weaving her way through the tables.

The poker room at the Collosio is huge, the biggest poker room in the United States. You'd think the biggest poker room would be somewhere in Vegas or Atlantic City, but nope, it's right here in Connecticut. There are more than a hundred tables filled with people playing cards, and even more people are standing around, waiting to get into a game. One of the best things about working the poker room is that it's quiet compared to the rest of the casino. No screaming slot machines. And it's smoke free. It's Thursday night, so I figured the place would be dead, but there are so many people I wonder how we're even going to be able to walk, let alone do it with these trays.

I try to keep myself from tripping as I weave my way through the tables. I'm not very good in high heels, and Adrienne wouldn't let me wear the shoes I had on (black Adidas gym shoes, which my older sister, Robyn, bought last year and then immediately stopped wearing when they became "uncool" a few months later) and made me wear black heels she borrowed from some other waitress, named Nancy, who had an extra pair. (Very shady, wearing someone else's shoes, because of toe fungus, bacterial infection, etc.)

"Mackenzie!" I yell, trying to get her to slow down. I step on a guy's foot, a middle-aged man with a gray beard who's sitting at a poker table. "Hey!" he yells. "Watch it!" My tray gets jostled, threatens to spill my plastic cups full of liquid all over the carpeted casino floor.

"Sorry," I say, but he's already turned back to his cards. This is definitely not part of "hanging." I take a deep breath, trying to practice the yoga breathing I learned in the Young Meditators group I was in last year. (Line from the Wellesley Web page under "admissions requirements": "Prospective students should be well-rounded, with a variety of extracurriculars." Which is so me. Completely well-rounded with a variety of extra-curriculars. And now I even have a job, yay!)

"What are you doing?" Mackenzie's a few feet

ahead of me, looking back in exasperation. "You didn't stop to write something down, did you?"

"Uh, no," I say, abandoning my breathing. "I'm just having trouble walking in these shoes." I hold my leg up as if to illustrate the insanity of having to carry heavy trays in high heels.

"You'll get used to it," she says, not sounding all that sympathetic. She puts her hand on her hip, her fingers curving around her slim waist. "Now come on." I follow her obediently. "Beverage," Mackenzie calls, zipping among the poker tables. "Beverage?"

"Beverage?" I say uncertainly, holding my tray and following her as best I can. "Bevvverragge?"

A man wearing a blue flannel shirt gives me a dirty look. Geez. Not too friendly around here, are they? But maybe it's because they take their poker really seriously. I would, too, if I was risking hundreds of dollars. Of course, I wouldn't be risking hundreds of dollars. That just seems stupid.

"You don't have to scream," Mackenzie hisses. She hands someone a soda and takes the dollar chip he hands her. She gives the guy a huge smile and drops it into her tip cup. "Thanks, honey," she says.

"Thanks, honey," I echo, trying it out and putting a little wiggle in my hips. Mackenzie rolls her eyes. "Less flirting, more concentrating on keeping your tray up. You're going to drop it."

"Oh, come on," I say. "I'm not that bad." Yeah, the tray is heavy, but I'm totally coordinated. In second grade I took gymnastics. We learned to do cartwheels and did a synchronized dance. "I used to be in gymnastics," I explain to Mackenzie.

"Yeah, well, you're not in Kansas anymore." This makes no sense, and I'm contemplating what she meant by it (that I'm out of my element? that I'll be desperate to get home after working here?) when I trip and fall, spilling my whole tray of drinks onto a dealer.

Oops.

♥　♠　♣　♦

He was perfectly nice about it. The dealer, I mean. Said it wasn't even his good work shirt. But still. How embarrassing. Not to mention one of the customers sitting at the table was totally annoyed. And I can tell Mackenzie is not too pleased with me.

"Shannon spilled some drinks," she immediately tells Adrienne during our break. We're in the employee lounge, where Mackenzie has produced some kind of yogurt seemingly out of nowhere. No one told me I was supposed to bring any dinner, and even though there's a little café in the casino, right around the corner from the poker room, I'm not sure I'm allowed out of Mackenzie's sight. Not to mention I probably shouldn't be spending seven dollars on a sandwich. Why didn't I remember to bring something to eat? Going hungry definitely can't be good for my working state. In fact, I think I'm starting to feel a little light-headed. You know, from all the heavy tray lifting and stress.

"Lovely," Adrienne says, writing something down on her clipboard. "How'd you do that?"

"I tripped," I say, wanting to blame it on the shoes she gave me, but not wanting to seem whiney. I wonder if she's going to fire me already.

But all she says is "Well, don't trip. And bring me a copy of your birth certificate. I need a backup form of identification."

"Sure!" I force my voice to sound bright and cheerful. I don't have a fake birth certificate. I wonder if I can get one. Fake IDs are one thing (everyone needs them to drink), but fake *birth certificates*? I've only heard of these in movies, when people go into some dark alley and get fake papers for secret spy missions. I'm not a spy. And I'm afraid of dark alleys.

Recap of the night so far:

Number of times yelled at by Mackenzie:
    seventeen
Number of drinks served: eight million
Number of drinks spilled: eight drinks at one time
Number of times butt was pinched by drunk
    poker-playing men: two
Number of times was asked to procure fake birth
    certificate, possibly causing me to get fired,
    have to find dark alley, and/or be arrested:
    one

For all this trouble, at the end of my five-hour shift, I will have made fifty dollars. After taxes, that works out to about forty dollars maybe? All this work for forty dollars. What a travesty. College textbooks can cost around a hundred and fifty bucks each. So I'll have made about a quarter of a textbook. Not even, when you factor in the cost of the uniform I ripped. I'll probably still owe *them* money.

Adrienne walks out of the room, toward the bar area, mumbling something about food costs, so I turn around to ask Mackenzie nonchalantly if everyone has to have their birth certificate on file (has spilling drinks made me seem suspicious?), but she's already left and is back out on the floor! Rude!

Number of new friends made at work: zero. Sigh.

♥　♠　♣　♦

By the end of my shift, my back is aching, I'm not getting any better at walking in heels, and although I manage not to spill any more drinks on people, I *do* spill a drink all over the floor in the bar area and almost cause one of the other waitresses, a girl named Tansy, to slip and fall and kill herself. (George, the bartender, catches her just in time, right before she goes down. She screams, "OHMIGOD, I ALMOST BROKE MY ANKLE!" and I apologize for ten minutes, but she won't forgive me. At all. I know this because she tells me. She says, "Sorry, but I won't forgive you. At all.") Mackenzie is so annoyed with me that she decides we're going to punch out three minutes early.

"You know, you'll get much better tips if you get a new attitude," she says as she slides her card through the punch-out machine.

"I don't know," I tell her, sliding my own card through. "Remember earlier when I tried to flirt? You yelled at me and then I spilled a big tray of drinks all over that man."

"You could learn," she says. She pulls her tips out of her tip cup, sits down at one of the tables in the break room, and starts to count them. The chips make a clinking noise as she stacks them up. "And if you don't want to flirt, just ask them about their poker playing, they love that."

"I don't know the first thing about poker." I sigh. I'm looking at the page in my notebook that has my Wellesley calculations on it. I subtract the forty dollars I made tonight, leaving the grand total of money still needed for my first year at $27,360. I tell myself that it's okay, that I'll start making more once I can keep my tips.

But how am I going to do this Every. Single. Night? Is this what people mean when they talk about the real world? If so, I'm definitely not ready for it.

"Whatever," Mackenzie says, checking her Black-Berry for texts and then sliding it back into her bag. "I have to go. Lance is meeting me and we're going to the concert upstairs."

At first I don't bother asking who Lance is. Probably her boyfriend. Then I realize this might be why I'm horrible at making friends. Because I don't take an interest in other people's lives. "Who's Lance?" I ask politely. "And what concert is it?"

"The Killers," she says, ignoring the question about

Lance. She seems like she's about to say something else, but she just shakes her head and gives me another look, like "OMG wow you're hopeless," and then turns on her heel and leaves. I decide to worry about her later, since I'm exhausted and have two hours of homework waiting for me.

I force myself up from the table and over to my locker on the other side of the room, where I place my borrowed shoes gently on the floor, lining the toes up against the wall. I hope their owner finds them. I cannot afford to buy her new ones after a fifty-dollar (forty-dollar) payday.

I seem to have lost the paper Adrienne gave me with my locker combination on it, and I'm definitely not about to go ask her for another one, so the combination takes me six tries, and when the door finally opens, a smooth cream envelope falls out. "Shannon" is written on the front in red cursive script. It's sealed, and the back is stamped with a picture of two playing cards, the ace of spades and the ace of hearts. I turn it over in my hand, praying it's some kind of employee-orientation thing or info on how to cash my paycheck. Then I have an awful thought: A pink slip?

I slide the paper out—one sheet—and am relieved that it's white. I think maybe pink slips are actually pink.

Dear Shannon,

Please come to room 2123 in the Grand Mahnan Tower Hotel of the Collosio Casino immediately to discuss an extremely important matter. If you choose to ignore this request, FURTHER ACTION WILL BE TAKEN.

I look around, half expecting to catch one of the waitresses hiding behind a table, a hand over her mouth to cover the giggles. But I'm all alone. I look at the letter again, hoping I'm not in trouble. There's no way they already could have found out I was working here illegally, is there? I mean, this letter isn't even signed and they spelled my name wrong. If they found out I was underage, wouldn't it be all official-looking and signed by someone with a scary-sounding title, like Head of Casino or Security Manager?

I'm tempted to just ignore it, because I really am completely exhausted and desperate to get home. But if it *is* something important, I don't want to be accused of skipping out on meetings on my first day. I already haven't made the best impression, what with the spilled drinks and my hips destroying one of their uniforms. So I sigh, shove my street clothes into my bag, and then head toward the elevator and the Grand Mahnan Tower Hotel.

2

There's a hot guy in the elevator, so I almost wait for the next one, mostly because I'm not that great around guys, especially hot ones. I haven't had much practice with them, and the ones I *have* had practice with haven't exactly left me with the best track record.

But then the elevator doors start to close and Hot Guy reaches his arm out to make them stop. Which is kind of sexy. I mean, his arm could have gotten cut in half. I totally saw something like that on Discovery

Health. And then he says, "Are you getting on?" and I have no choice but to step in, because to say no would make me look like a complete loser and/or a lunatic, because why wouldn't I want to get on the elevator when I was clearly and obviously waiting for it?

"Thanks," I say.

"No prob," he says. He has his cell phone out, and he's scrolling through his texts.

I sneak a look at him out of the corner of my eye. Floppy dark hair, baggy jeans, a leather jacket over a faded gray T-shirt with some band name on it I've never heard of. His face is scruffy, and he's holding a pair of dark sunglasses in one hand, his cell in the other.

We don't say anything at first, which is kind of awkward. At least, it is for me. Probably not for him—he doesn't look like the kind of guy who feels awkward about things. I'm contemplating whether I should say *something*, or at least maybe pretend to look at my own texts, but then, right around the seventh floor, he laughs loudly at something on his phone.

"Funny text?" I say, because it seems like maybe he wants me to remark on it, and also because, you know, anything is better than silence.

"You have no idea," he says, still scrolling. He doesn't offer any more information. Alrighty then. The numbers in the elevator are going up super-slowly, inching their way to twenty-one. Ten, eleven . . . Seriously, what is up with this elevator? I hope it's not broken. I don't think I'd do very well being stuck in here. "I'm Cole," the guy finally says, holding his hand out.

"Shannon," I say, taking it. Wow. He has big hands. Mine gets totally enveloped in his, and I say a quick prayer that I don't have sweaty or disgusting palms from all the drinks I served tonight.

"So what are you up to tonight, Shannon?" he asks. But he's already gone back to looking at his phone, now scrolling through what look like his e-mails.

Something tells me that "Um, nothing" is probably not the coolest answer, nor is "I have to get home, because my parents don't know I'm working at the casino." And even though he's just some hot guy in the elevator who I will probably never see again, I don't want him to think I'm a loser, so I just smile and say, "On my way home."

"On my way home" could mean anything. It could mean that I'm going home so that I can change and go out to the clubs. It could mean "on my way home to call my hot boyfriend." It could mean "on my way home to my fabulous apartment, where I live alone and throw tons of fab parties" or it could mean "on my way home to . . ."

"Then why are you going *up* in the elevator?" he asks. He slides his phone into the pocket of his jacket and looks at me.

Oh. Right. "I have a, uh, business meeting," I say, a little more defensively than I intended. But honestly, what's with the twenty questions? I mean, what is he, the Elevator Police?

"In room 2123?" he asks. "Yeah, that's where I'm going, too."

"You work here?" I ask, surprised. Most of the dealers I've seen tonight are older. The one guy I saw who was even remotely around my age was wearing pink socks, had a double ear piercing, and spoke little to no English. But maybe Cole isn't a dealer. Maybe he's a waiter in one of the restaurants, or maybe he works security.

"You have no idea," he says again, and smiles as if to say, "Isn't this place crazy?" He has a nice smile. Nice teeth. White and straight. I smile back.

Number of potential new friends at work: one. One very hot guy, which might actually count as two. At least one and a half, definitely. Yay!

The elevator pings at floor twenty-one, and we both step out.

"So where do you—" I start, but before I can finish, his hands are suddenly on my back, hard and strong, and he's pushing me roughly toward the room across the hall. The door to the room is propped open by something, and he pushes it with his free hand, taking me with him.

"What the *hell*?" I say, not sure what's going on. He pushes me again, and I catch a glimpse of a plaque that says "2123" outside the door, and then I'm stumbling and tripping into the room, totally off balance.

I look around, praying this is some kind of work-place prank, but as my eyes adjust to the darkness (and smokiness, eww) of the empty hotel room, it only takes me a second to realize this isn't a joke, and that following an anonymous note left in my locker was definitely not one of my smartest ideas. And then I hear the sound of Cole shutting the door behind me. Okay, I think, don't panic. My heart starts pumping in my chest and I turn around to try to get the hell out of there.

But Cole's blocking my way, and the click of the dead bolt latching echoes through the room. "Relax," he says. "I just want to talk to you."

In movies, when someone just wants to talk to you, it means they just want to kidnap, kill, or rape you. Or maybe sell you into slavery. So I open my mouth, reach deep into my lungs, and scream.

I surprise even myself with how loud it is.

"Whoa, whoa," Cole says. He reaches behind him, unlocks the door and holds up his hands. "Relax, relax, I'm not going to hurt you."

I reach into my bag and pull out a can of hair spray. I wrap my hand around the base and swing it at him. "Stop!" I say. "I have Mace."

"That's hair spray," Cole says, ducking as he moves past me, further into the room. My wild swing doesn't even make contact.

"It is not," I say. "It's Mace." But my voice falters. Cole sits down on the bed, then takes his jacket off and throws it over the chair in the corner.

"Chill," he says. He pulls a cigarette out from behind his ear, picks a lighter up off the table by the bed, and lights it. He takes a long drag and then blows smoke rings into the air.

I narrow my eyes at him and glance at my now-clear path to the door. I take my phone out and slide it open, just in case I need to dial 911, and look around the room for something I can use as a weapon. Why oh why didn't I take a self-defense class instead of stupid Young Meditators? But now that the path to the door is open, my heart rate starts to slow down just a little bit.

"Seriously, Shannon Card," Cole says, studying me. "You need to learn how to relax."

"Relax?" I practically scream. "You pushed me into your hotel room and now you want me to *relax*?" Does he not watch *48 Hours Mystery*? They always start somewhere sketchy, like a casino or a hotel room. A hotel room in a casino is like a double whammy. "And how do you know my last name?" I cross my arms at him in what I hope is a threatening manner.

"I didn't push you in here," he says. He rolls his eyes like he thinks I'm being super-dramatic. You know, like I'm some crazy girl freaking out over her boyfriend wanting to hang out with his friends on a Saturday night or something instead of the fact that some crazy guy is attempting to kidnap her. "You came in of your own accord."

"No, I didn't," I say. "You grabbed me in the hallway and pushed me in here." I open the door and check the little sign outside. Yup. Room 2123. "You," I say, "were waiting for me in that elevator."

"No one forced you to follow my note," he says. He leans back further on the bed and blows another smoke ring toward the ceiling.

"I thought it was some kind of employee meeting!" I say. "I didn't know you were a psycho who wants to *kill* me!"

"I don't want to kill you," he says.

"You want to sell me into slavery, then," I say.

"Is that what you think?" he asks. "That I want you to be a slave?" He stabs his cigarette out in the ashtray on the table next to him and gives me a cocky grin like "Oh my God, you are so naïve and funny."

"Whatever," I say, turning the doorknob again and pulling the door back open.

"Hey, wait, wait," he says, standing up. "I'm sorry, I'm sorry." I stop but keep one hand on the doorknob.

"Do not," I say, "come any closer!" I hold the hair spray out. It may not be Mace, but I could definitely whack him in the head with it. Or at least spray it in his eyes until he was writhing around on the floor in pain.

"Okay, okay," he says, holding his hands up. He takes a step back. "Listen, I don't want to kill you or hurt you or sell you into slavery."

"Then what do you want?" I ask.

"This is you, right?" He pulls a crumpled-up piece of paper out of his pocket. He's still a few feet away, but I can tell what it is. An Internet printout of an article from our local newspaper, the *Whitinsville Eagle*. HIGH SCHOOL JUNIOR WINS BIG AT MATH DECATHLON, it says. It's accompanied by a picture of me smiling into the camera and looking a little cross-eyed. Also, I'm wearing a white shirt, which has the unfortunate effect of making it look like my head is floating in midair.

Uh-oh. Is this some kind of trick? Is Cole actually casino security, trying to fool me into admitting I'm only seventeen? I square my shoulders and pretend I have no idea what he's talking about.

"No," I say, squinting at the picture and hoping I look super-confused. "I've never seen that girl in my life."

"It says your name underneath it," Cole points out. Damn.

"What do you want?" I ask again, letting the door go. It closes behind me. "If you're trying to blackmail me, good luck with that. I have seventeen dollars to my name, so if you want to go through all this trouble for *that,* then be my guest!" I pull open my purse and shake my money onto the ground in a pathetic storm of fives and ones. I was trying to sound haughty, but it didn't come out that well. "And where did you get that print-out, anyway?"

"Googled you," he says.

"Why were you Googling me?" I ask suspiciously.

"We do a standard background check on all the new employees."

"We?"

"Aces Up."

"What's 'ay says up'?" I ask. Definitely sounds shady.

"It's a poker society," he says. "And we want you to join."

I frown. "A poker society? I don't know anything about poker."

"We want to teach you." He looks at me intently, his dark eyes serious. "We think with your math skills, you might be able to win a lot of money."

"How much?" I ask in spite of myself. I mean, I would never gamble for money. a) I can't risk losing everything. b) Gambling is shady. And c) I'm underage. Lying to get a job is one thing. Lying to gamble is another thing completely. But still. Now that Cole doesn't seem as dangerous, and my path to the door is clear, I'm slightly intrigued.

"Lots." In this light, he looks a little bit like Casey Affleck. But I will not be swayed by mopsy hair and dimples. Especially when I'm smart enough to know that nothing comes for free, especially money.

"Yeah, well, assaulting me outside the elevator? Not the way to get me to join your stupid society," I say.

"Aces Up is secret," he says, waving his hand like it makes perfect sense. "We have to be careful who sees us together."

"I don't want to be a poker player," I say. I open the door again, and my feet sink into the soft carpet of the hallway. "I don't want to be a gambler of any kind.

And so I'm leaving." I take one step outside, waiting for him to call after me or at least threaten to tell I'm underage. "Aren't you going to try to stop me?" I ask, turning back around.

"Nope," he says. And then he looks me up and down, like he's sizing me up. But not the way guys usually do, like they're trying to figure out if they want to hook up with you. It's more like he's giving me a try-out of some sort. In fact, it's kind of . . . sexy. Way sexier than the other kind of sizing up. But then I remember there's nothing sexy about accosting me in an elevator and trapping me in a hotel room.

And then I figure it out. He's pretending he doesn't need me, so that I'll be all, "I want to be a famous poker player, oh, please please please!" Ha! He obviously doesn't know who he's messing with. "I'm leaving," I say again, forcefully this time.

"Okay." He shrugs. Annoying.

"Well," I say. "Bye." I step all the way into the hallway then.

"Bye, Shannon," he calls as the door shuts behind me. But something about the way he says it implies that he thinks I'm going to be back.

3

*T*he whole drive home, my head is spinning. This is *definitely* the craziest thing that has ever happened to me. Should I be scared? Flattered? Should I call the police? I mean, being accosted in an elevator? You totally hear about those kinds of things on *Real Stories of the Highway Patrol.* Well, maybe not that show *exactly,* because obviously the highway patrol wouldn't be patrolling the casino. They patrol highways. But some show like that. (*Real Stories from Casino Security?*)

Anyway, what would I tell them? The police, I mean. That a guy left a creepy note in my locker, kidnapped me, and then let me go without hurting me? I'd have to give them a statement for sure, and since I'm a minor, they'd definitely have to get my parents involved. Everyone would find out I'm underage, and it would be a whole big mess. Still, though. If it's a choice between getting caught at the casino and getting killed, I'm all about getting caught.

I'm so preoccupied that at first I don't notice that the kitchen light in my house is on, shining through the blue and yellow plaid curtains. Uh-oh. Who would be in the kitchen this late? My mom's been working at Starbucks to make extra money, and she has to be there every morning by four, so she's usually in bed by ten at the latest.

My dad is trying to keep his "internal clock on a good schedule" by getting to sleep early and getting up early to job hunt, and my sister, Robyn, never hangs in the kitchen, preferring to stay in her room, IM'ing or talking on the phone with her boyfriend, Leonardo. Crap, crap, crap. They're probably all awake, having some big family meeting about me and my lies.

I rack my brain for a good excuse about how or why I was at the casino tonight. Picking up a friend? Doing undercover research for a class assignment? Yes! Doing undercover research! For a paper for my human behavior class. Studying the behavior. Of humans. At the casino.

I speed up, anxious to get the whole scene over with. But as I get *closer*, I realize there's a car with flashing lights in our driveway. Ohmigod! The police are here! The casino has probably called the police on me, and now I'm going to be arrested! But when I pull into the driveway, I see that it's not a police car at all, but a tow truck, its orange lights flipping all around and bouncing off the blackness of the driveway. I park my car next to it and cut the engine.

"What's going on?" I demand, stepping out of the car. A guy wearing blue overalls with the name Butch stitched onto the pocket is loading my dad's BMW coupe onto the back of the truck. Then I notice my sister, Robyn, standing on the front porch. Her long hair is in her face, and she's hugging her arms to her body. Her eyes are puffy, and her cheeks are flushed, like maybe she's been crying.

And then I get it. Robyn took my dad's car out (probably without his permission, for some kind of party, which she's been known to do—hello, who wouldn't want to take a BMW to a party?), and now she's crashed it and she's in total trouble.

"Are you okay?" I ask Robyn, abandoning Butch and rushing over to my sister. "Did you get hurt?" I scan her for bumps and bruises and scratches. But her face is clear and flawless, as always. I breathe a sigh of relief. Now that I know she's okay, I start to think that this whole car-crashing thing might not be so bad. I mean, my parents are definitely not going to care that

I'm home a little later than anticipated if Robyn crashed the car. That's way more scandalous.

"Hurt?" Robyn asks. "Why would I get hurt?" She's wearing one of my dad's old Harvard sweatshirts, and the big maroon arms flop around her slender body.

"Because you crashed the car," I say. I look at her face to assess if we need to do any sisterly ESP. Usually we're pretty good at figuring things out without even speaking, like the time Robyn missed the SATs because she slept through them and I completely covered for her without even knowing the story.

"I didn't crash the car," she says.

"What's the story?" I ask, leaning into her. Better get it straight now, before I go inside, so that my parents can't bombard me with any surprise questions.

"The story?" she repeats.

"Yeah, the story, what are you telling them about how it happened?"

She grabs me by the shoulders. "Shannon. I. Did. Not. Crash. The. Car."

"Then who did?" Is it possible my dad crashed it? That seems totally unlikely, since my dad is seriously the slowest driver *ever*. One time it took us an hour to get to my grandma's house twenty minutes away. My dad's not even that old, but for some reason, he loves to go ten miles under the speed limit.

"No one," she says. "The car's fine."

"Then why is it getting loaded onto a truck in the

middle of the night?" I turn around and watch as Butch slowly attaches the wheels of the car to the truck. I peer closely at it and realize that it looks fine. Not a scratch or a ding on it. Hmmm. Butch really doesn't look all that friendly. He has a very cranky expression on his face, and I almost expect him to have a hook where his hand should be.

"They're taking it," Robyn says. I give her a blank look. She sighs. "They're repossessing it."

"Repossessing it!" I say, a little louder than I intended. Butch glances up for a second, glares at me, and then goes back to loading up the car. Wow. A lot of menacing things are happening tonight. I lower my voice. "What do you mean *repossessing* it?"

"They're taking it," she says again. She slides a hair tie off her wrist, then gathers her dark hair into a ponytail.

"But *where*?" I ask. "And *why*?"

"Away from here," she says. "And because, you know, Mom and Dad couldn't pay for it anymore."

"Away from here," I repeat, imagining my dad's nice new car being shipped off to some . . . I dunno, *car lot* somewhere, with a bunch of other cars that people couldn't pay for. A lump rises in my throat, and I swallow it. Obviously I knew my parents weren't doing that well, since my dad lost his job. But I had no idea that people were about to start *taking* things from them. That's horrible.

"Why are they doing it at eleven o'clock at night?" I ask.

"That's when they do it," Robyn says. "I just happened to be coming home in my own car and ran into him."

"Where were you?" I ask.

"At Leonardo's," she says. "We were fighting again. About the pants."

"Sorry," I say, reaching out and squeezing her hand.

Robyn and her boyfriend have this ongoing feud about leather pants. About a month ago, Robyn and Leonardo were watching a music video on MTV (in our family room, I might add, while I was trying to use the only computer that's available to me in the house to write an English essay) in which some girl was wearing these super-tight leather pants. Leonardo declared that the pants were "bangin' hot."

The next day, my sister borrowed a similar pair from her friend Stacy to wear to this party they were going to. Unfortunately, although he was a big fan of them on the girl in the video, Leonardo seemed to think *Robyn's* pants were "skanky." Robyn then decided that Leonardo wanted to keep her covered up like some sort of Middle Eastern woman, and told him they were in America and she could wear whatever she wanted, and no, she was not going to put on jeans and a sweater. Now whenever they get in a fight, the pants come up. Which doesn't make much sense, but whatever.

"How was your first night at work?" Robyn asks. I can tell she wants to change the subject.

"Um, it was fine," I say. "Kind of stressful, you know?" Understatement.

"What," she says, her eyes widening, "are you wearing?"

Oh. Whoops. I'm still wearing my cocktail waitress uniform. After I found that note in my locker, I was in such a rush to get upstairs that I didn't take the time to change. I didn't think it would matter, since I wasn't expecting anyone to be up when I got home. Obviously I wasn't counting on a car-repossession situation throwing the house into a state of activity.

"Oh, um," I say. "This is my work uniform." I give her a grin, like "Isn't it so cute?" Robyn's eyes widen as she takes in the plunging neckline, the built-in push-up bra, and the tight waist. Good thing I left the heels at work.

"They make you wear that at a *diner*?" she asks. "That seems a little . . . racy, doesn't it?" Robyn and my parents think I'm working at the Rusty Nail, a twenty-four-hour diner that's about half an hour away.

"Not really," I say. "It's, uh, you know, in Stamford." I roll my eyes, like we can't possibly understand the ways of the big-city folk in Stamford, but my sister looks skeptical, and my stomach ties itself into a guilt-filled knot. Which is a horrible, horrible feeling. I have never kept *anything* from my sister before. Ever.

But there are multiple reasons I can't tell her about working at the Collosio:

a) I really don't want to put Robyn in the position of having to keep something from my parents. Covering for someone for one night while they're out at a party is one thing, but deceit that could last for months, about something that is totally illegal? So not cool.

b) Robyn was supposed to go to UConn before my dad lost his job, but now she's spending her first semester of school at the community college. It wouldn't be very nice if I told her I was trying to make money for Wellesley when she's not able to be at the school she wants.

c) I feel slightly guilty about keeping the money I'm making to use for school. Especially now that things are getting taken from us! I mean, shouldn't I be helping my family? I'm hoping that by the time school rolls around, my parents will be back on track. Still. Suddenly, it seems totally selfish.

"It really doesn't seem like they should expect you to wear something like that," Robyn says, still focused on my uniform. "Is your boss a guy?"

"Um, no," I say. I reach into my bag, take out the sweater I was wearing earlier, and pull it on over my uniform. Now it just looks like I'm wearing a sweater with a black skirt. "It's a girl, she just—" I try to think up a reason any female in her right mind would make someone wear something like this. "She used to work in the circus, and so she's super into costumes."

"She used to work *where*?" Robyn asks, frowning.

The front door to the house opens, and my dad sticks his head out, saving me from any more questions. I say a silent prayer of thanks that I pulled my sweater on before my parents noticed my outfit.

"Girls," he says, "do you want to come in so we can talk about this?"

We trudge into the kitchen. My mom's at the table, a cup of tea in front of her. I sit down in the chair next to her, and Robyn hoists herself onto the counter.

"Now," my dad says. "I don't want anyone to worry. The BMW was a car we didn't need, and the fact that it's gone isn't going to affect our family in the slightest." Um, even I know this isn't *exactly* true. I mean, yeah, I guess no one really *needs* a BMW, but it was my dad's *car*. How is he going to get around? As if he's reading my mind, my dad says, "I can drive your mother to work in the mornings, and then pick her up in the afternoons. That way, I'll be able to use the car during the day for any interviews, appointments, et cetera, I might have."

Robyn and I glance at each other, and I can tell we're thinking the same thing. But it's Robyn who has the courage to say it out loud.

"Are we . . ." Robyn fiddles with one of her rings and averts her eyes. "What about the house?"

"We are not," my mom says firmly, "losing our house."

My dad nods. But honestly, who knows whether they're telling us the truth? If we *were* losing the house, there's no way they'd tell us. I mean, up until a few minutes ago, if you'd told me I'd come home to find some guy named Butch loading our car onto his truck, I would have thought you were nuts.

"Girls," my dad says. "Really, I don't want you to worry."

My parents spend the next ten minutes trying to reassure us that everything is fine, and that we really shouldn't be worried, and that my dad has a great lead on a job from his friend Hank Blumenthal over at Farber Bank, and that every family has tough times, and blah blah blah. They're just getting to the part about how proud they are of us for cutting back on things without complaining when Robyn's cell phone starts ringing.

"It's Leonardo," she says after checking the screen. "I'm, uh, going to take it. But don't worry, Dad, honestly, because I'm not worried." She gives him and my mom each a kiss on the cheek and then heads upstairs to her room. She's not fooling me. She's totally worried. Which is why she took the phone call. If she *wasn't* worried, she would have stayed here to talk about it.

"So," my mom says brightly. "Now that we're all awake, how about I make some more tea and we can talk about your first night at work?"

"Um, well," I say. "There's not that much to tell." This may be the biggest lie I've told so far. Maybe even ever in my life. I try to think of something I can extract from the night that would be parent appropriate. "I mean, it was interesting." Totally not a lie. "I spilled a drink on a man." Also not a lie.

"Oh, honey." My mom sets two teacups down, one in front of me, one in front of my dad. I pick out a decaffeinated bag from the bowl in the middle of the table. My nerves are way too shot for caffeine. "That's okay, it was only your first night. You know that when I was a waitress, I—" She stops talking then, a confused look passing across her face, and for a second I panic, thinking maybe she somehow knows my secret.

But then I hear it. Screaming coming from Robyn's room at the top of the stairs.

"Well, if you weren't such a jerk!" Robyn's shrieking. Her voice sounds like one of those people in bad karaoke YouTube videos that get passed around the Internet. A silence comes over the kitchen as my parents try to hear what Robyn and Leonardo are fighting about.

"We really shouldn't be listening to this," I say. "It's spying." Suddenly, I'm starving, and I get up and head to the cupboard to grab a snack. This has been a completely crazy night, and I deserve some junk food. Not to mention I didn't even have any dinner.

"No, that *is* true!" Robyn's voice comes shooting down the stairs. "Because you *said* that those pants were skanky!"

My dad's eyebrows shoot up, and his green eyes glint with excitement. I sigh. My dad is so obviously hoping that Robyn and Leonardo are going to break up. He's like one of those sports fans who paint their faces the team colors and write "GO PANTHERS" on their chests, even though the other team is favored by a bazillion points.

Although I can't really blame him for not liking Leonardo. I mean, he's not a likeable character. He eats with his mouth open, and he walks into our house without even ringing the doorbell and then goes, "Hello? Hellllloooooo?" like he's been out there knocking for hours. One time he walked in while I was lying on the couch in just a T-shirt and a pair of underwear. (No one else was home.) I'm not sure what was more embarrassing: being caught with no pants on, or the fact that he didn't even try to sneak a peek.

"They're not going to break up, Dad," I say, shoving a handful of chips into my mouth.

"Honey, why don't you have some of that baked ziti in the fridge?" my mom asks. "You should eat something more than just chips." My mom gets confused by the idea of snacking. She doesn't understand why people would opt for a snack instead of a good meal. She's probably right about chips not being the best late-night dinner, though. I did split a seam at work tonight. "Did you eat at the Rusty Nail?" she asks.

"Noooo," I say truthfully. Suddenly, my throat feels tight, and I put the chip I'm holding back into the bag.

"How about a grilled cheese?" my mom presses. "Wouldn't you like one of those?"

39

"I'm fine, Mom," I tell her. Well, I was. Until some crazy guy accosted me and my dad's car got taken away, all in one night.

"Why are you so sure they won't break up?" my dad asks me, his bushy eyebrows knitting together in confusion. "They're fighting about the pants again."

My poor dad doesn't get that relationships (especially teen relationships) don't follow logic. He's definitely more of a numbers/hard data kind of guy, which is why it's so sad that he lost his job, since it was perfect for him. He would get so happy taking the train every morning into New York, where he'd spend his days working as an investment banker, playing with numbers and stocks and whatever else investment bankers do.

Until his whole company went under, and my dad lost his job and most of our savings, which were tied up in company stock. The weird thing is, even though we're essentially broke, my dad still does have *some* stocks, and the value of our house is still so high (even though it's nowhere near what we paid for it) that I'm not going to be able to get as much financial aid as I need for school. Which is another reason I can't tell my parents I'm working at the Collosio. My dad would feel super-bad if he knew my debauchery was partly because he can't find a job.

"Yeah," I say to him now, trying to be gentle. "And they've been talking about the pants for what, weeks now?"

"Yes, but maybe she'll get fed up with it, like it's the last time," my dad says hopefully.

"Maybe," I say, even though I don't believe it. But I have to be nice to him, because my dad's had a hard night, and anything I can do to give him hope is important.

The sound of something heavy hitting the floor comes from Robyn's room. My dad looks toward the ceiling, his face turning even more hopeful as it becomes apparent that Robyn is either stomping around or throwing things.

"No, you can't come over," Robyn yells. "It's midnight and my dad's car just got repossessed and I need to *go. To. Sleep!* I know, I know. . . . I love you, too, but it's *late at night!*"

My dad sighs and adds two huge spoonfuls of sugar to his tea. "She's saying, 'I love you,' " he says sadly. "And he wants to come over."

"It's okay," I say. "Maybe next time." I reach over and give him a pat on the hand.

"I dunno," my dad says dejectedly. "Things might go on like this for a while." And I'm not sure if he's talking about Robyn and Leonardo or everything else.

♥ ♠ ♣ ♦

The next morning. School. I'm waiting for Chris Harmon at his locker before first period, since I need to ask him about getting me a fake birth certificate. It's 7:56, and the bell is going to ring in ten minutes. I rushed to get here early, watching my rearview mirror the whole time to make sure no one was tailing me, either a) wanting to repossess my car or b) making a second attempt to get me to join some shady poker society.

Although I do feel a little better after spending more than an hour last night Googling "Aces Up." There wasn't that much info, but from what I could gather, Cole was telling the truth. They're a secret poker club that has cells all over the country, and its members apparently get together and pool their money in an effort to win big. There was nothing about them killing people or luring innocents into hotel rooms. But still. You can never be too careful.

You'd think getting to school early would give me plenty of time to ask Chris about a birth certificate. I mean, the conversation should go something like this:

Me: Chris, do you make fake birth certificates?
Chris: No.
Me: Okay, thanks anyway. (Goes to freak out and break into hives.)

or alternately:

Me: Chris, do you make fake birth certificates?
Chris: Yes, when do you need it by?
Me: The sooner, the better.
Chris: Okay, that will be x dollars and I'll have it to you by x.
Me: Thanks. (Does happy dance down the hall.)

But conversations with Chris never really go this way. Not that I've had that many. Pretty much the only time we've interacted was when I got my fake ID from him. (Well, if you don't count the times in seventh-grade study hall when he used to snap my training bra and laugh his head off like it was the most hilarious thing since *Best Week Ever.*)

Anyway, during our fake-ID conversation, Chris had a hard time wrapping his head around the fact that I wanted an ID for a job. He kept asking me what bars I wanted to go to, and I kept telling him it was for a job, but he still didn't get it. ("A job? You mean like a . . . *stripper job*?") Finally, when I told him it was for the casino, he rolled his eyes and said, "Why didn't you just tell me you wanted to gamble? Jesus, it's not like I'm going to tell anyone."

I check my watch: 8:57. Come on, Chris, I think. Get your ass in here. And then I see Max Heller loping down the hall toward me. Oh. My. God.

How could I have forgotten that Max's locker is right next to Chris Harmon's? Of all the mornings for me to be having an encounter with Max Heller, this has to be the worst. My hair is not combed, I am wearing light blue fleece pants and a white T-shirt, and I have forgotten to put on socks.

I didn't get much sleep last night (probably because of the strange encounter I had with a hot poker-playing thug and the realization that my parents are in BIG TROUBLE and my whole family might be one step away from homelessness), and as a result, my hair is a mess, my clothes are wrinkled, and I will probably have blisters due to improper footwear.

I look around for a door I can slip through, or a hallway I can duck into, but it's too late. Max is standing in front of me before I can get out of there.

"Hey," Max says.

"Oh," I say. "Hi. Um, I'm just waiting for Chris Harmon. I have to ask him something." I shift my bag from one arm to the other and look down at the floor.

"Cool," he says, sounding slightly uncomfortable.

"I have to ask him something about a birth certificate," I say, deciding to be more specific.

I do not want there to be any doubt in Max's head about who I'm waiting for, i.e., I do *not* want him to think that I am waiting for him.

This is because Max Heller and I have a bit of a . . . history, I guess you would call it. Max and I used to be BFFs. Last year, when I was a junior, we had this great friendship. We had fun with each other and told each other everything, and even though we spent almost all our time together, there was none of that weird "will they or won't they get together" vibe that seems to permeate every teen drama on The CW.

We were just friends.

But then, on the last night of the summer, we were both at a party (Robyn's friends were throwing it, and since I was her little sister, I got to tag along and I brought Max with me), and somehow Max and I ended up alone on the back porch, and I don't even remember what we were talking about or how it happened, but suddenly there was this . . . electricity in the air, and we kept moving closer and closer to each other, and right at the very end of the night, I thought he was going to kiss me. But he didn't, and I spent the whole ride home in Robyn's car trying to convince myself I'd imagined it, and that Max and I really were just friends.

But then Max texted me later that night at around two o'clock in the morning and was like, "That was a really fun night, I def should have kissed you," and then I texted back, "Why didn't you?" and he said, "Did you want me to?" and I said, "Yes," and then he said, "Next time." I couldn't sleep all night, and I spent like five hours getting ready for the first day of school, the next day, and when I showed up, it was super-awkward and Max said hi to me but then kind of acted like I didn't exist.

Since then, um, we haven't really spoken.

"Cool," Max says now. He shrugs, but he also looks slightly alarmed, like he's afraid I'm here to confront him and go all psycho girl, ranting and raving about how he never called me or talked to me. (Full confession: I *have* been tempted to do that. I really have. But I do have some pride, so I've totally been able to resist. Well. There might have been a few times when Robyn had to spend hours talking me out of confronting him, and once when my phone had to be taken from me and locked in the trunk of her car. But that only happened once. Or twice.)

Max starts opening his locker, and I turn and look down the hall. Damn. What am I supposed to do *now*? I can't just *leave,* because then he's going to know that I'm leaving because he's here. And besides, I really need that birth certificate. But if I stay, I'm going to have to make conversation with him, and honestly, what would we talk about? Somehow "How have you been?" doesn't seem like it would work. Neither does "What ever happened to that kiss you were going to give me?" or "Hey, remember when we were friends?" God. I really, really wish I'd brushed my hair.

"So," Max says, "are you, uh . . . are you doing that tutoring thing?" He still sounds a little worried.

"What tutoring thing?" I ask, my head spinning from his closeness. Which kind of makes no sense, since until that night last summer, I never considered him anything more than a friend. But now apparently everything's switched and I can't help noticing how hot he is.

"There's this tutoring thing," he says. He's wearing a blue hoodie with a big yellow *M* on it. Looks like a school logo. Michigan, maybe? His short dark hair is a little wet. But not gel-like wet. More like he just got out of the shower. Thinking about Max in the shower makes me blush, and I'm reminded of the time last year when Robyn, Max, Leonardo, and I all went swimming in Leonardo's pool. Max has a six-pack. I take a deep breath and force my thoughts away from a shirtless Max.

But I *still* can't help noticing how hot he is. Deep hazel eyes. One crooked bicuspid, which is totally sexy, like Matthew Fox from *Lost*. His forearms look tan and strong as he takes the books he needs for the morning out of his locker. "Ms. Kellogg is asking for some volunteer tutors to help people who are having trouble."

"Are you going to tutor?" I ask politely.

"No, um, I'm looking for a tutor," he says.

"You're having trouble in calculus?" I ask, kind of shocked. Max is very smart.

"Sort of," he says. He looks at the ground, like he's embarrassed. It's weird that after we were so close he'd feel embarrassed telling me that he's having trouble in calculus. It makes me sad, and for a second, I don't say anything. "I, uh, just want to make sure I get at least a B, so I don't screw up my transcript." The bell rings, signaling the beginning of first period, and Max slams his locker door shut. "Uh, I don't think Chris is coming," he says.

"Me neither," I say dismally. Damn. What am I going to tell Adrienne now? She doesn't seem like the type who's easily put off by excuses.

We're walking down the hall together now. Me and Max. Walking. Together. For the first time in months. Although we kind of had no choice. We're in the same first-period math class, so unless one of us wanted to take the long way around and risk being late, we had to walk together. I mean, I guess one of us *could* have made some excuse, like we had to use the bathroom, or that we forgot something in—

"Anyway," Max says. "So, uh, would you ever . . . would you ever think about tutoring me?"

"Tutoring you?" I repeat dumbly. Oh. My. God. Max Heller is asking me to TUTOR HIM. Is he a little crazy? Does he not remember what happened between us? Are Max Heller and I going to forget about our past and maybe become friends again? Until one day in a few weeks, when we're looking over some equations, I'll lean in, and Max will say, "I like the way you say 'x.' I've always thought it was really sexy, ever since junior year." And then I'll say, "You mean like this? 'Exxxxxxx,' " and then Max will lean over and—

Wait a minute. "Wait a minute," I say. What about Parvati? "What about Parvati?" Parvati Carlson is Max's girlfriend. She is also my math archenemy.

"What about her?" Max asks, frowning, like Parvati is the last thing on his mind. Which makes no sense, since they've been dating for two months. Yup, Max got together with Parvati about two weeks after our near-miss kiss. Which is one reason I've never bothered to ask him about what happened between us. I mean, when a guy almost kisses you and then starts dating someone else, it's kind of clear how he feels.

I say calmly, "Why don't you ask her to tutor you?"

"Thought of that," he says. "But we probably wouldn't get much done."

Oh. Right. Of course he wouldn't ask his girlfriend to tutor him. They'd probably get carried away and start making out. Or even having sex. My stomach flips as I think of something else. If he can't have Parvati tutor him because they will immediately start having sex, does that mean he wants me to tutor him because he *doesn't* want to have sex with me? Is that why he didn't kiss me last summer? Because I am unkissable and unsexable?

Well, he can forget it. I am nobody's not-having-sex tutor. I am nobody's you-won't-tempt-me-so-it's-okay-to-hang-out-with-you tutor. Max Heller can fail math for all I care. In fact, I hope he fails math and then flunks out of school. And ends up on the streets, and then someone will ask him where it all went wrong, and he'll be like, "I expected Shannon Card to be my you-won't-tempt-me-so-it's-okay-to-hang-out-with-you tutor and she turned me down and now I'm ruined."

"So, what do you say?" Max Heller looks at me with his beautiful hazel eyes under his long eyelashes and smiles at me with his crooked bicuspid.

I sigh. "Okay."

"Great," he says. "There's a meeting after school today. Anyone who's interested is supposed to go."

"Well," I say. "Uh, how long is the meeting?" I have to be to work at three, and I can't afford to be late on my second day.

"Probably only an hour or so," he says. We're at the classroom now, and he stops and leans against the wall outside. "Parvati says these things don't usually last that long."

Ugh. How does Parvati know? This is the first time we've had an informational meeting about tutoring, and in my experience, informational meetings *always* run long and get very boring. At the informational meeting for Young Meditators, we meditated for half an hour *after* all the information was given. Total waste of time.

"Um, well," I say, "I might have to call my boss and ask her if it's okay if I'm in a little late to work."

"You have a job?" He frowns.

"Yes," I say, and decide not to offer any more information. He's not the only one who's going around creating a whole new life for himself. I have a job that he knows nothing about. I wonder what he would think if he knew I'd been invited to join an underground poker society. Probably he'd be shocked. I'm not sure if I imagine it, but I think I see a look of sadness flash across Max's face. We're standing pretty close together now, and I can smell his mint shampoo and laundry soap. I shiver.

"You cold?" Max asks. He frowns again.

"Uh, no," I say brilliantly. "Are you?"

"No," he says. "I'm actually a little hot." Oh, God. I'm starting to feel light-headed.

"Hello!" Parvati Carlson pops her head out of the math room. Max looks startled.

"Oh," he says. "Uh, hi." She walks over and loops

50

her arm through Max's. At least he has the decency to look slightly uncomfortable.

Important things to know about Parvati:

1. She always matches. As in, her clothes, her accessories, her shoes . . . You would never catch her carrying a black purse with a navy blue outfit. Today she's wearing a green polo shirt, a green and pink striped flippy skirt, a green headband, and white sneakers.
2. She has a weird way of making you feel bad about yourself: bragging about her accomplishments and, at the same time, pretending to be totally embarrassed by them.
3. No matter what kind of news you have, or how long you've been talking to her, she always turns the conversation back around to herself.

"Are you ready for the test?" Parvati asks. She smiles sweetly. Parvati is also a big fan of double meanings. Like she'll pretend to be your friend, but you have to really look deep into what she's saying to figure it out. For example, "Are you ready for the test?" sounds completely innocent, right? But it's not. She really means that she wants me to fail miserably.

"I hope so," I say. This isn't true. I actually think I'm going to nail the thing (my brilliant math aptitude plus my hours of studying and ability to focus under immense pressure), but I can't let her know that.

Whoever gets the highest grade in calc this year receives a five-thousand-dollar scholarship to the school of their choice, courtesy of Arthur Peabody, some rich guy who used to go here. Parvati and I are pretty much neck and neck for the scholarship, so we do this thing where I downplay how well I'm doing and Parvati tries to get in my head by bragging about how well she's doing. It's all completely infantile, but somehow necessary. (The weird thing is I don't even like math. I want to major in English and creative writing. But my best subject is math. So the Peabody Scholarship is my chance to score a little extra money for Wellesley, where I'll be free to write short stories to my heart's content and leave my graphing calculator at home in my sock drawer, if I so choose.)

"Okay, so, like . . . ," Parvati says. She studies her perfectly manicured fingernails. She leans in close. "I think I'm going to do really, really well on it."

"Good for you," I say. Parvati does not need a scholarship. Parvati has two horses, private tennis lessons, three small dogs and wears a new pair of shoes every day. However, her family is totally into her getting the scholarship, because they want the "prestige." Her word, not mine.

"Also," she says, "Ms. Kellogg? She pulled me aside this morning and was like, 'Parvati, you have to join the tutoring program, because you're one of the best students we have.' " She smooths the bottom of her hair and then slides her other hand up and down the strap of her green messenger bag. "She's giving me two people." Parvati says "two people" like she's completely embarrassed that Ms. Kellogg asked her to tutor to begin with, and even more shocked that she was asked to tutor two students.

"That's awesome," I say. Because that's the thing about Parvati. You can't really be mean to her when she's doing her whole "aw, shucks" routine. Otherwise you're the one who ends up looking like a jerk.

"Did Max talk to you about doing it?" she asks. She smiles up at him, her face glowing. Ugh.

"Uh, yeah," Max says. "I just asked her, and she, uh, she said yes." At least he's stuttering. I can't help but feel happy that he's uncomfortable.

"That is so cool," she says. "I've been bugging him to do it. You're the only one I would trust, Shannon." She smiles like she's being nice, but it's obvious what she means: she doesn't want him spending time with any of the hot girls in the class, like Abby Marsh, who wears boy-shorts underwear as gym clothes. She obviously doesn't know about our near-miss kiss. "So you'll be at the meeting?"

"Yes," I say. "As long as my boss says I can be a little late to work."

She nods, like it makes perfect sense that I would now need a job. "How's your dad's job search going?"

"Good," I lie. I have no idea how she knows my dad lost his job. Maybe Max told her? We were still friends when it happened. I look at him, but his face is blank.

"It's just so horrible, all this financial stuff," Parvati

says. "I'm so stressed out about it. I can hardly eat, like, my size fours are just *falling off* me." Parvati comes from old money; she's the kind of rich that ensures that even if her family took a big hit, she would still be more than fine. I resist the urge to stab her with my pencil.

"So, ah, I guess I'll call my boss now," I say in an effort to refocus my thoughts. "You know, to make sure it's okay that I go to the meeting."

"Okay," Max says. He takes Parvati's arm and tries to steer her toward the classroom.

"See you later, Shannon!" she calls over her shoulder.

"Totally," I say, giving her a huge fake smile. I head into the bathroom to call Adrienne, since we're not supposed to be on our phones at school. Also, I don't want Adrienne to hear any sounds in the background that could be associated with high school, like lockers slamming or bells ringing.

I barricade myself in a stall and scroll through my phone until I find Adrienne's cell number, which she gave me at my interview two weeks ago. ("You are to use this number for call-ins only! *CALL-INS ONLY,* AND NOT IF YOU HAVE A WORK-RELATED QUESTION THAT CAN WAIT UNTIL YOU SEE ME!")

"Oh, good morning, Adrienne," I say when she answers. "This is Shannon Card calling."

"*Who?*" She sounds like she might have just woken up. Which, now that I think about it, is probably true. She works nights. So why would she be up so early? Whoops.

"Shannon Card," I say. "You know, your new star cocktail waitress?" I'm trying to be funny (obvi), but Adrienne doesn't really seem to appreciate the joke.

"Why are you calling me at this hour?" she demands. I hear a rustling noise on the other end of the line, like she's rolling over, and then a deep groan. Gross.

"I'm calling," I say, "because it's been brought to my attention that I will not be able to arrive at work tonight until four o'clock." Please don't ask me why, please don't ask me why, please don't—

"Fine," she says, her voice still deep. "Is that all?"

"Um, yeah," I say. "That's all." That's it? Much easier than I expected.

"Don't forget your birth certificate." And then the line goes dead. *Right*.

At least if I get fired, I won't have to worry about my tutoring interfering with my work schedule.

*B*y the time I leave school, I *still* haven't heard from Chris Harmon. I don't think he's a very good businessperson, running a business where you can't even get in touch with him. If there was a Web site where you could go to rate the person who got you your fake ID, I would definitely leave him a bad rating. Seriously, this is not any way to do business. Next time I will be getting my fake documents from someone else, for sure.

Not that I know anyone else who does fake documents. But he can't be the only purveyor of fake documents in town; that would be ridiculous.

Anyway, now I'm going to have to spend the night avoiding Adrienne. The good news is I didn't even have to worry about being late for work, because Parvati was right. The meeting lasted about fifteen minutes. And it was a total waste of time. Ms. Kellogg went over the expectations, and we all had to sign a sheet saying who we were going to tutor. And that was about it. Although one super-embarrassing thing *did* happen. When the meeting started, Ms. Kellogg was all, "Oh, Shannon, here, I have your shirts," and handed me two T-shirts that said "YOU CAN COUNT ON ME–I'M A MATHEMATICIAN!" I won them a few weeks ago during a raffle for the math club. But if you didn't know that, it seemed like I bought two dopey T-shirts about math. Ugh.

When I get to work, I rush into the dressing room. I'm hoping I'll have a few minutes before work starts to talk to Mackenzie. I want to ask her about Cole and Aces Up.

But when I get into the dressing room, Mackenzie's standing in front of the mirror in the communal area, looking at herself and putting on mascara. And sitting on the sink, watching her, is a guy. A very cute guy, in one of those scruffy I'm-in-a-band-and-your-parents-would-probably-hate-me kind of ways. But still. There's a guy. In the girls' changing room.

"Oh," I say. "Um—"

Mackenzie rolls her eyes at my obvious discomfort, like she can't believe how totally immature I am for thinking it strange there's a guy in here. "You don't have to freak out, Shannon," she says. "It's just Lance."

As if its just being Lance makes it any less sketchy that there is a boy in the girls' dressing room. I mean, I don't even know him. Not that Lance could see me changing or anything. We have separate stalls for that. But still. How am I supposed to ask Mackenzie about Cole now? Not to mention that if Adrienne finds him in here, she'll flip out.

"I'm not freaking out," I say coolly, pretending to just go with it.

"Yo," Lance says, giving me a little salute. He's wearing silver rings on every finger. Cool.

"Yo," I say back, because it seems appropriate. Then I just stand there. I'm not really sure if I'm supposed to go in and change, or if I'm supposed to wait until Lance leaves. I walk over to the sink and start washing my hands, mostly because I have to do *something*.

"So that's why I think we should go," Mackenzie says. "Everyone is going to be there, and Krista's sister will definitely be able to get us in." She leans forward and pouts at herself in the mirror.

"Honey, how are we going to afford that?" he says. He's reading a magazine—it looks like *Rolling Stone* or something—and he flips the pages fast, barely glancing at them. "You know that drinks alone are going to cost at least a hundred bucks."

"Don't worry," Mackenzie says. She pulls the front of her uniform down, exposing a huge amount of cleavage, along with a small sparkly butterfly tattoo on the top of one breast. "I'll work on getting extra tips tonight."

I pull a paper towel out of the dispenser and dry my hands. I wonder what Lance is going to think of Mackenzie's exposing her boobs like that.

"Sweet," he says, and pulls her toward him, giving her a big kiss on the lips. Well. I guess that answers that question. Eww.

"So I guess I'll go change now," I announce loudly once they've pulled apart and Mackenzie goes back to applying her makeup. I throw my paper towel into the garbage can with a flourish.

"You know, Shannon," Mackenzie says, turning away from the mirror and looking at me thoughtfully. "It wouldn't hurt you to show some cleavage, too." She looks me up and down. "You'd get much better tips. Don't you agree, Lance?" She turns around and looks at him, waiting for the verdict.

Lance nods. I don't have time to think about the appropriateness (or inappropriateness) of some other girl's boyfriend deciding whether I should show cleavage, because Mackenzie has pulled a bra out of her bag. A very padded, very sexy, very red bra. "This," she declares, holding it up by its strap, "is what you *should* be wearing."

I don't point out that I really don't want to take fashion advice from Mackenzie, since right now she's wearing sparkly black shoes with five-inch heels and straps that crisscross up her ankles, her boobs are hanging out of her dress, and she has six pounds of makeup on. Not that she doesn't look great, because she does. But she also looks like she's on her way to amateur night or *Pussycat: The Search for the Next Doll* auditions. "Thanks," I say. "I'll keep that in mind." I give her a smile like I really mean it, and hope that's the end of the conversation.

She holds out the bra to me. "Take it," she commands.

"You want me to wear *this one*? Right now?"

"Oh, come on, Shannon, it's clean," she says. Not what I was worrying about, but good to know.

"You totally should," Lance says, licking his lips. He has a tongue piercing, and the stud glints in the light. "You would look totally sick."

Mackenzie nods. "But not as sick as me, right, honey?"

"No, no one is as sick as you," Lance declares. Then he reaches over and smacks her on the butt. I'm not sure if I should be insulted, but then decide no, since a) she is his girlfriend, and b) she *is* definitely sicker than me.

I sigh, then take the red lace bra from Mackenzie and check the tag: 34B. Thank God. I'm a 36B. "This is the wrong size," I say, shrugging as if to say, "Oh, well, we tried, better luck next time, haha."

"Doesn't matter," she says. She leans close to the

mirror and wipes some purple shadow over the tops of her eyes. "It'll still push you up, and it'll be way better than that granny thing you're wearing now." She wrinkles her nose in disgust.

How does she know I'm wearing a granny thing? Is it that obvious? Could Max tell I was wearing a granny bra? Could Parvati? Are my boobs sagging? I pull my shirt tight and look at my boobs in the mirror. Hmm. I guess maybe I do look a little . . . frumpy.

I sigh and take the bra into one of the changing stalls. I pull my clothes off, ball them up into my bag, put the bra on, and then throw my uniform on over it. Wow. This thing really does push your boobs up, and it isn't all that comfortable. Then I realize that there's no mirror in here, which means that if I want to see what I look like, I'm going to have to venture out.

Maybe after Mackenzie and Lance leave. Yes. That's a good idea. I'll just hang out in the stall until they leave. Five minutes later I'm still standing in the stall while the two of them talk about a litany of things (the weather, Mackenzie's new dress, which she got on sale for forty dollars, and some situation involving a stolen car and their friend, who, from what I can tell, is named Chicken). This is a horrible plan.

"What's taking you so long?" Mackenzie finally demands.

"Yeah, we want to see what it looks like," Lance chimes in. Oh, Jesus.

"It doesn't fit," I try.

"Nice try," Mackenzie says, leading me to believe she's smarter than I previously thought.

I sigh and open the door. I catch a glimpse of my reflection in the mirror over the sinks. Not as bad as I expected. My boobs are definitely pushed up and out, but not to the point of threatening to give everyone a peek.

"Hot," Mackenzie says.

"It's okay." Lance shrugs and goes back to his magazine.

"Thanks," I say, rolling my eyes at him.

"But you need some makeup," Mackenzie says.

Ten minutes later, I'm on my way out to the floor, with my hair brushed, my boobs out, eyeliner applied, and lips glossed.

"There you are," Adrienne says. "I've been looking all over for you."

"Oh, hi," I say. Damn. Figures I would run into her first thing. I grab my tray from the table and start loading it with drinks.

"You look good," she says.

"Thanks." Although I'm not sure this is a good thing. If Adrienne and Mackenzie think I look good, does that mean I don't? Today Adrienne is wearing tight black leggings, a short fitted black skirt, and a tight black T-shirt that plunges so far down I feel like I can almost see her belly button. The outfit isn't that bad, I guess, but she has black lipstick on. And black eyeliner. And her nails are painted black as well. Very

Elvira scary. Although I think Elvira has red lips. Anyway. The point is if these two think I look good, does it mean I do look good, or that I look, as Lance would say, "sick"?

"Anyway," Adrienne says, obviously through with being nice. "I need your birth certificate."

"Oh, right," I say, as if I've totally forgotten about it. I reach down to grab a couple more cups of water to add to my tray, and the top of my push-up bra peeks out of my dress. Oops. I push it back down with one hand.

"So where is it?" Adrienne demands.

"Uh, it's in my locker," I say. "Is it okay if I get it for you at the end of the night? I don't want to leave Mackenzie in our section all alone."

"Fine," she says. "But don't forget." And then she disappears.

"Hey, Mackenzie," I say once Adrienne's gone and we're almost finished loading our trays. "Can I ask you something?"

She nods, but she's already walking down the hall toward the poker room. I rush to keep up, being careful not to spill my tray. Fast walker, that Mackenzie. She's like some kind of acrobat in her heels.

"Do you know a guy named Cole?" I try to keep my tray steady. A mini-bottle of water falls over, and I quickly stand it back up, thankful it has a cap.

She frowns. "Cole who?"

Good question. "Um, just this guy, Cole," I say.

"He's about eighteen or nineteen, I think he hangs out here a lot, kind of looks like Casey Affleck."

She seems confused for a second, but finally she says, "I think I showed him and his friends my tattoo once." She pulls down her dress, showing off the sparkly butterfly.

"You showed them your tattoo?" I ask, confused. "So you know them?"

"Yeah," she says, waving her free hand like it's nothing. "I mean, no, I don't *know* them know them. But they're here a lot. So I've seen them around." She looks at me and knits her fake eyebrows. Well, at least I think they're fake. They look like she pencils them on. I'd never have the nerve to do that. What if you didn't have time to draw them on one day? Or what if it rained and your eyebrows starting dripping off? Hopefully her eye pencil is waterproof. "Why? Do you like one of them? The scruffy one, what's his name?"

"Cole," I answer. "And no, I don't like him. I just . . ." I consider telling her what happened last night. She might know something I don't. But I'm not sure I can trust her, and besides, what if she makes me tell Adrienne? The last thing I need is people asking me a bunch of questions, and I really do *not* want to see Adrienne again tonight if I can help it. "It's nothing."

And then I push Cole and the crazy happenings of last night out of my mind and force myself to focus on my shift.

5

As soon as work is over, I change out of my uniform and then run out of the casino and into the parking garage before Adrienne has a chance to ask me about my birth certificate again. And when I say I run, I mean I *run*. Literally. So I'm kind of out of breath by the time I get to the parking garage, and my fingers are shaking as I dial Chris Harmon's cell number.

To my surprise, he answers on the first ring. I've been looking for him all day, and now he answers. Apparently he's not a fan of normal business hours.

"Yo," he says. "Who dis?"

Who dis? Jesus. "Um, hi, Chris," I say. "It's Shannon Card." Silence. Okay, then. I decide to just put it out there. "I need a, uh . . . I need a document." I'm sitting in my car now, my eyes scanning the elevator doors that lead to the casino, just in case Adrienne decides to chase after me. Unlikely, but, you know, better safe than sorry.

"I know," Chris says, sounding bored. "Max told me."

"He did?" I ask, and my heart skips. Max mentioned my birth certificate! Which means he totally believed me this morning when I told him I was waiting for Chris! I wonder what Max thought I needed the birth certificate for. Is Max worried about me? Was he asking about me? Was he trying to dig up information about what I've been up to? "That was nice of him," I say, trying to sound nonchalant. "Did he say what I needed it for?"

"Max doesn't do my business," Chris says, sounding upset that I would even imply such a thing. "I do."

"Oh, of course not," I say, not wanting to make him mad, since he's my one and only link to fake forms of identification. "I didn't think Max did any business for you."

"Anyway, I have it," he says.

"You have my fake birth certificate?" Relief floods through my body.

"Yeah," Chris says. He lowers his voice to a

66

whisper. "Listen, we probably shouldn't talk anymore about this on the phone."

"Okay," I say, getting nervous that he's going to hang up and I'll never be able to get in touch with him again. "But I really—"

"Can you come and meet me?" he asks.

"Right now?"

"Yeah, I'm at the IHOP near school, having some breakfast." As if to prove this, he starts to chew something noisily. Who eats breakfast at ten o'clock at night? Is he just starting his day?

"Okay," I say before I can think about it or he can change his mind. "I'll be there in twenty." Then I decide it's definitely best to clarify. "And, um, you have my birth certificate, right?"

"I always," Chris says wisely, "keep things on my person."

And then he hangs up without saying goodbye. Wow. He has a real sparkling personality, that Chris Harmon. I check the clock: 10:07. Okay. Twenty minutes to IHOP, five minutes to pick up the birth certificate, and then ten minutes home. I should be home by eleven, giving me just enough time to study for my math quiz tomorrow.

But when I try to start my car, the engine won't turn over. I push the key in again and keep trying it, again and again and again, but the car just sputters and then dies. Every. Single. Time. Crap, crap, crap. I take a deep breath and lean back in my seat. Okay. Think.

Who can I call? My family is obviously out, since they'll wonder what I'm doing at the casino.

Triple A? Except I don't *have* Triple A. I let my membership expire after I'd gone six months without using it. I figured it was a waste of money. Of course now I need it. That's how it always works. The same thing happened with my laptop. I didn't get the insurance plan, and a few days later I dropped it and cracked the screen, and I couldn't afford another one, so now I have no laptop. Ugh.

I'm contemplating going back into the casino to see if Mackenzie is still around when someone knocks on the driver's side window of my car.

I jump. Oh. My. God. It's Cole. Cole is outside, in the parking lot, knocking on my car window. He motions for me to roll it down, and even though there's a feeling of trepidation inside me, that's what I do.

"Hello," he says, giving me a big grin.

"Hello," I say warily.

"Miss me?" he asks, still grinning.

"No," I say. "I just saw you yesterday, when you creepily dragged me into your hotel room." He puts a pouty look on his face, then grabs the top of the window frame and leans in close. He smells like cigarette smoke. I make a motion like I might start rolling up the window and crush his fingers between the glass and the frame. I guess that's one advantage to not having power windows: you can finger crush even if your car won't start.

"Hey, hey, hey," he says, releasing the window frame and pulling his fingers back. "Calm down. I just wanted to see if you needed any help."

"I don't," I lie, mostly because I'm still slightly scared of him and want him to go away.

"It looks like your car won't start," he says.

"That's not true," I say. "My car's fine."

"Then why aren't you going anywhere?"

"I was just sitting here for a minute, waiting for my . . . uh, my head to clear before I got on the road." I give him my most charming smile.

He looks doubtful. "Waiting for your head to clear?"

"Yes," I say haughtily. "My job is very stressful."

"Then you should come work for us," he says.

"No thank you," I say. I stare straight ahead.

Cole waits for a minute, then walks away, disappearing into the rows of cars. Phew. That was a close one. I mean, he's obviously crazy. Then again, aren't all gamblers? They're always trying to pay off their gambling debts by cooking up some kind of crazy scheme. And most of them are one step away from losing everything. I read all about gambling addictions last night while I was clicking around the Internet, Googling "Aces Up."

I pull my cell phone out of my bag and think that it might really be time to call the police. I mean, knocking on my window like that? That's pretty creepy. But again, what would I tell them? A guy happened to be

69

walking through the parking garage and offered to help me start my car? This whole thing is too weird.

Then I see a black Ford pickup truck pulling up behind me in the rearview mirror, and when I turn around, Cole is stepping out of it. Okay, deep breath. What was it they taught us in that self-defense unit in gym class? Go for the eyes? Or was it the throat?

Cole taps on the window again. "Pop the hood," he says. His voice is muffled through the glass, and I crack the window slightly so I can hear him. "I'm going to give you a jump start."

Oh. Well. My phone vibrates in my hand before I can decide what to do, and my mom's cell number pops up on the caller ID. Damn. I consider sending it to voice mail, but if I don't answer, she's liable to do something crazy, like drive to Stamford and turn up at the Rusty Nail looking for me.

"Hello?" I say into the phone.

"Hi, honey," she says brightly. "Just wanted to make sure you were on your way home from work before I hit the hay!" Oh, God.

"Yup," I say. "Just on my way home from work." I do my best to match her happy tone.

Cole walks around to the front of my car and taps on the hood. "Open up!" he says. "And pop the trunk, too, so I can get the jumper cables."

"Who's that?" my mom demands. "What is he saying?"

"Oh, that's just a guy I work with," I say. Which

70

isn't exactly a lie. Cole spends a lot of time at the casino, and I work at the casino, so we do kind of work together. I fumble around until I find the latch that releases the hood, and then hit it.

"What's he doing?" my mom wants to know.

"Um, he's just . . . he's trying to get this one cabinet open, the one that has the condiments." I hold the phone away from my mouth and say, "Oh, yes, Bob, good, I was wondering where that ketchup went."

My mom's not stupid, so she says, "I don't believe you." And then she says, "Put him on the phone."

Oh, for God's sake. "He can't talk to you," I say. "He's busy working. Which is what I should be doing right now, so that I don't lose my job."

"I thought you said you were on your way home," she says.

"Well, I didn't mean *literally*," I say. "Like, I'm not actually driving, I'm just about to get on the road."

"Who are you talking to?" Cole asks, coming back over to my window. "I'm going to try to jump it, so I need your jumper cables."

"Are you having *car trouble*?" my mom shrieks. And then she says, "I'm coming down there!"

"Mom, no!" I say. "That's just . . . I mean, my friend Bob is here, and he's helping me."

Cole raises his eyebrows at me. "Aren't you, Bob?" I say pointedly.

"Oh, yeah," he says into the phone. "Bob's helping right out."

"Let me talk to him," my mom says again.

"No," I say. "Mom, look, it's fine, I'll be home soon, I promise."

"Okay," she finally says, relenting. "But if you're not home in twenty minutes . . ."

"I will be," I say, and hang up before she can say anything else.

Cole's got the hood open now, and he's standing by the side of the car, looking at me through the windshield with a very amused look on his face. "Your mom?" he asks.

"That," I say, "is none of your business." I keep my phone in my hand, just in case. "Look," I say, "thanks for your help, but I've got it from here."

"Do you have jumper cables?" he asks, ignoring me.

"No," I say.

He looks at me incredulously. "You don't have jumper cables?"

"No," I say, challenging. "Do you?"

"I'm not the one driving a car that's two steps away from the junkyard." Gasp. What a jerk. "Do you at least have Triple A?" he asks. I consider lying, but then I realize if I don't let Cole help me, I might just be stranded here.

"No," I say miserably, and wait for him to make another dig about how horrible my car is.

But Cole just walks to the front of the car and lowers the hood. He reaches into the pocket of his jeans

72

and pulls out a cigarette, lights it, and then takes a slow drag, the smoke drifting lazily toward the ceiling. He reaches back into his pocket and pulls out his cell. He dials a number and says, "Hi, I'm having a little car trouble, and I need a jump." He pauses, then looks at me. "It's a—"

"A 1997 Corolla," I tell him.

He finishes the call and snaps his phone shut.

"Thanks," I say.

"No problem." There's an uncomfortable silence. I sigh and finally get out of the car, then stand awkwardly by the driver's side door.

"So, you can probably go now," I say. "I'm fine here, honestly. I don't mind waiting."

"I have to stay until they get here," he says. "Because I'm the one that has the Triple A card." He blows a long plume of smoke up to the ceiling, then hoists himself onto the hood of my car.

"Feel free," I say, trying to make him feel bad about sitting on my car without asking me if it's okay. But he just grins. I sigh again, then sit down on the hood next to him and try to console myself with the fact that if he wanted to kill me, he would have done it last night when he had me alone in his hotel room. Not to mention there are cameras all over this place, including the parking garage, so it'd be pretty dumb of him to try anything.

"It's going to be two hours before they get here," he says.

"Two *hours*?" Where the hell are they coming from? Saudi Arabia?

He shrugs. "I guess they're busy."

The door to the parking garage opens, and a bunch of girls come out of the elevator, giggling. They look like they're half drunk, and they're falling all over each other.

"Hey, Cole," one of them says as she walks by.

Cole gives her a long look, his eyes moving up her body. "Hey, Marissa," he says. For a second she looks like she's going to say something else, but then she keeps going. I inexplicably feel jealous.

"Who was that?" I ask.

"Just a friend," he says lightly. Then he winks at me.

"You know . . . ," I say, jumping off the hood and facing him. I cross my arms and look at him. "You're kind of an ass."

He pretends to be shocked and then hurt. He puts his hand to his heart over his leather jacket. His fingers are dirty from trying to look under the hood of my car. "I *am*?" he asks.

"You can't," I say, "just go around following people out to their cars." Seriously. What is *wrong* with him?

"I thought I was helping you," he says. "And I didn't follow you. This is a public parking lot."

I consider mentioning that it's totally piggish to be scamming on girls who are wandering through the parking lot in scandalous body-baring clothing, but I don't. I check my cell phone for the time: 10:23. Which means we've only been waiting for about seven minutes. A hundred and thirteen more to go. Sigh.

There's no way I'm going to be meeting up with Chris Harmon now, so I text him and ask him to meet me before school on Monday. Actually, I command him. I tell him I'll meet him at his locker before the first bell. I hope Cole thinks I'm texting my boyfriend, some super-big guy who plays college football and is coming down here to take care of him and make sure he doesn't mess with me anymore. Then I text Robyn and tell her that my car won't start and I'm waiting for Triple A with a guy I work with, and ask her to please take care of Mom. She texts back, "No problem," with a smiley face. Thank God for sisters.

Cole reaches into the pocket of his jacket and pulls out a deck of cards. He starts shuffling them, his hands moving back and forth. He's wearing a silver ring on his thumb, and the overhead lights bounce off it as his hands move expertly through the deck.

He sees me watching him, so I become haughty. "If you're trying to seduce me into your card-playing world, it's not going to work."

He doesn't answer, just holds the cigarette out to me and offers me a drag. "No thanks," I say. Is he crazy? Doesn't he know smoking is disgusting and causes all sorts of horrible diseases, not to mention it makes you smell all smoky and gives you yellow teeth? Of course, Cole doesn't have yellow teeth. He has very white teeth. But not too white, not in an "I whiten my teeth" kind of way. I hate that. And the smoke on him doesn't smell gross. It smells kind of . . . dark, if that makes any sense. Dangerous. But almost in a good way.

Cole takes another slow drag off his cigarette. "I'm not trying to seduce you into anything," he says. And then he looks right at me. "Card playing or otherwise."

"Funny," I say. I roll my eyes because I can't really think of a good retort. I feel cold, so I go to my trunk and pull out a sweatshirt. Cole is dealing the cards now, putting five piles of two cards in a circle on the hood.

"What are you doing?" I ask.

"Playing poker," he says.

"With yourself?"

"Practice," he says. "To run different combinations in my head, and see if I can win or not." He looks at me. "It's math," he says. I watch as his hands move the cards around, flipping them over, shoving them back into the deck, dealing them faceup on the car.

"Do you want me to teach you how to play?" he asks, not looking up.

"What makes you think I don't know how to play?" Talk about being cocky. Then I remember that I told him last night that I didn't. So I quickly add, "I could have just said that to throw you off track."

"Do you?"

"Yes," I say. "I've watched it on TV before." This isn't exactly true. I mean, I *have* watched poker on TV a few times, when it happened to be on in the background, or when Leonardo somehow took control of our remote and wouldn't give it back. I know what beats what and the types of hands (two of a kind, flush, et cetera). I have no idea how the actual game works.

But Cole just raises his eyebrows at me, ignores what I just said, and then explains the game to me. Here's how it works:

Each person at the table is dealt two cards. A round of betting ensues, in which each person can either fold their hand or stay in the pot by putting in chips. After everyone has a chance to bet or fold, the dealer places three cards faceup in the middle of the table. These three cards are called the flop, and they're community cards; everyone can use them. So, for example, if you have a two in your hand, and another two comes on the table, you'll have two twos. Based on these new cards, everyone still in the game either bets, checks, or folds. The dealer places another community card faceup in the middle of the table. This one is called the turn. Another round of betting ensues, and then the last community card, called the river, comes up. Everyone who's still in the hand bets or folds, and then whoever has the best five-card hand using any combination of the five on the table and the two in their hand wins.

"Okay," Cole says when he's finished giving me the overview. He jumps off the car. Then he reaches into his pants pocket and pulls out a money clip. He peels five hundred-dollar bills off the top and holds them out to me. "Here," he says.

I look at him incredulously. "What's that for?"

"Take it and play," he says. "We have a couple of hours."

"In *there*?" I ask. Now I know he really is crazy. The guys at the poker tables are scary. They drink and they yell and they stay there for hours and sometimes they look like they want to kill somebody. They're obviously very unstable, betting thousands of dollars at the drop of a hat. There's no way I'm going in there and actually *playing*. Especially when I've never even done it before.

"Best way to learn how to play," he says, "is to just get in there and do it." He raises his eyebrows again, challenging me.

"What's the catch?" I ask, suspicious.

"No catch," he says. "Whatever you win at the end of the night, you get to keep." I hesitate. I *could* really use the money. Especially since God knows what's wrong with my car and what it's going to cost to fix it. But I'll have no clue what I'm doing, and the whole thing is completely and totally shady. Still, it's not like I'd be using my own money. And it might be better than standing out here with Cole for two hours. "It's also a good way to figure out if you have what it takes," Cole says. "If you're really going to be as good as we think you are."

78

Well, that settles it. I snatch the hundred-dollar bills out of his hand and start walking toward the elevator, Cole following behind me.

♥ ♠ ♣ ♦

I try to stall by stopping in the bathroom, and then I try to stall even more by buying a bottled water from one of the stands near the shops.

But Cole is insistent that I'm going to play, and when we get into the casino, he whispers, "Don't play anything higher than three-six," and then disappears. Like, literally disappears. Before I can even ask him what that means! Which is so totally not cool. I mean, shouldn't there be some kind of training program or something? Where he sits with me and mentors me for at least the first hand? They would never just leave you on your own the first day at a real job.

I head over to the cashier and hand her the five hundred dollars, my hands shaking. "Just some one-dollar chips, please," I say. "And, um, I guess some fives." I have no idea if this is right, but I figure you can't go wrong with one-dollar chips. They're like one-dollar bills. Good everywhere.

The cashier, an older woman with bushy black hair, whose name tag says "Flo," takes my money wordlessly, counts it out into piles, and then slides a huge rack of chips over to me. I pick it up and make my way through the tables over to the sign-in desk, where you go to get assigned to a poker table.

"Oh, hello," I say nonchalantly to the pit boss who's

running the desk. I wait for him to look up and say something like "Wow, aren't you a waitress here?" But he doesn't even recognize me. Or at least, if he does, he doesn't say anything. Maybe he's used to it. Employees of the Collosio are allowed to play bingo and poker here only, so maybe it's not, like, an unusual enough occurrence to remark on.

"Can I help you?" he asks, sounding bored. Wow. I might have to bring this up to Adrienne. The customer service around this place is totally lacking.

"Yes," I say. "I'd like to get into a three-six game, please." I try to sound confident, like I do this all the time. "Um, but just out of curiosity," I say, "what is a three-six game, exactly?"

"It has to do with the stakes," the pit boss says. "You can only bet three dollars after the deal and the flop, and then six dollars after the turn and river."

"Oh, right," I say. That makes total sense. "I just forgot for a second, haha."

The guy looks over his wire-rimmed glasses at me, and for a second, I worry that he's going to ask to see my ID. And he does. "Can I see your ID, please?" he asks.

"Uh, sure." I reach into my purse and pull my fake license out of my wallet. The guy studies it for a minute, then hands it back to me. "You can sit at table forty-seven," he says.

"Oh," I say. "Uh, there's no wait? Because, really, I'm not in a hurry or anything, I don't have to–"

"Table forty-seven," he repeats, more forcefully this time. Alrighty, then. I gather up my chips and make my way through the tables to number forty-seven.

The table isn't full; there are only about four or five guys sitting there, so I just pick a seat and plop myself down. I'm not used to carrying a big rack of chips, and I sit down a little too hard (the seats are low), and the chips go spilling onto the table. Whoops.

"Oh, sorry," I say, picking them up and putting them back into my rack. "Guess I'm not used to this, hahaha!" I pick up some chips that fell onto the floor, and when I pop back up, a guy wearing a flannel shirt at the end of the table gives me a grin. Actually, I think I know that guy. He looks very familiar.

Ohmigod. He was here last night when I dropped that tray of drinks! He was totally pissed! He said now he was going to reek of alcohol, and his wife didn't like him to be drinking on work nights, so then I said couldn't he just be honest with her and say that a waitress dropped some drinks, and then *he* said obviously I didn't know his wife, so then *I* said no, I didn't, but—

"Big blind," the dealer says, looking at me. Um, what? I stare blankly, having no clue what he's talking about. "Three dollars," the dealer says, sighing.

"Oh, right," I say, and give a laugh like I can't believe I forgot. I throw three dollar chips into the middle of the table. I figure out quickly that the blinds are forced bets, money that you have to put into the pot to keep it going. Kind of like an ante, only you don't have to put it in every time. They rotate, depending on where the button is.

The button is this little plastic disk that's sitting on the table, and I know from watching on TV that it moves from person to person after each hand. So if you're sitting to the left of the button, you must have to put in the small blind (which in this game is one dollar), and the person to the left of the small blind must have to put in the big blind (which in this game is three dollars).

Of course, Cole never mentioned anything about buttons or blinds or anything, you know, *important* like that. Figures. I mean, the guy is a complete jackass. He's probably lurking around right now, watching me to see how I do, if I'm thrown off by the fact that he neglected to mention two obviously important parts of the game. But I'm not rattled.

The dealer sets two cards in front of me, and I pick up the edges of them and look, careful not to let anyone see what they are. No way do I want anyone to know what I have; I know some people at this casino are very shady, and will try to get a peek at your cards no matter what. I've seen it in action, firsthand.

Hmmm. A queen and a king. "Pass," I say brightly when it comes around to me.

"You mean 'check'?" the dealer asks. He sighs again and looks up at the ceiling, like he can't believe I got stuck at his table. Seriously with the customer service in this place. Shouldn't they be making new players feel welcome?

"Right," I say. "Yes, definitely, check." That's right. In poker, if you want to pass, you say "check." The three cards the dealer throws into the middle of the table, the flop, are two, three, seven. All different suits. None of that helps me, so when it's my turn, I fold.

Boring.

The second hand is a little bit better, as I'm dealt two sevens, and the flop is seven, king, queen. All hearts, which means that someone could have a flush (five cards of the same suit, which would beat my three sevens), and I run the percentages in my head, figuring out that there are thirteen hearts in the deck. With three of them on the board, that leaves ten in the deck, and someone would have to have two of those ten to get a flush.

The turn is a three of diamonds, and at this point, everyone is out of the hand except me and the guy in the flannel shirt. The river is the two of spades. I bet, throwing my chips into the pot. The flannel-shirt guy raises my bet. That jerk! I know you're not supposed to let your emotions get involved in poker, but still. I mean, how dare he? I call his bet, and when we turn the cards over, he has a pair of kings. I win a pot of almost forty bucks.

Forty dollars! For ten minutes of work!

The dealer pushes the pot over to me, and I squeal with delight, "Forty dollars! Yay!" I can't help it. Can you imagine if I'd been playing the bigger stakes? Like five hundred dollars or something? I would have made thousands! Wow. Poker is fun.

"Nice pot, sweetheart," the guy next to me says. He smiles at me, and I smile back. The guy in the flannel shirt gives me a dirty look. Wow. Whatever. I mean, way to be a sore loser.

An hour and a half later, I'm up two hundred bucks. Two hundred dollars! Playing three-six, which is, like, the lowest stakes you can play. I'm actually starting to get the hang of this, *and* it is very, very fun. Plus everyone at my table is so friendly!

So far I've made friends with three other players: a nice businessman from New York, a college kid named Stuart, who's majoring in politics and is very smart (but he's a little nerdy for my tastes, *and* he has a girlfriend), and a perfectly nice but possibly shady man who keeps saying, "Booyah!" every time he wins a pot.

"You're on a roll, huh, Shannon?" Stuart says as I win twenty more dollars.

"Must be beginner's luck," I say. I mean, they're supposed to think I'm ditzy and crazy. Actually, I think they *do* think I'm ditzy and crazy, because a couple of times when I made certain calls or bets, I caught them all glancing at me and at each other with surprise. And the guy in the flannel shirt is definitely annoyed with me every time I take his money. Oh, well. If you can't take the heat, then don't sit down at the tables, you know?

I'm just about to throw in the small blind when I hear someone at the table behind me yell, "This drink is weak sauce!" in a loud, familiar voice. The familiar voice of someone who could get me in a lot of trouble.

I swallow hard. Okay, I think, don't panic, you don't know for sure that it's him.

I take a deep breath, lean in close to Stuart, who's sitting on my right side, and whisper, "Excuse me, Stuart?"

"Yeah?" he says. You're not supposed to whisper with other players during a hand, but since we haven't looked at our cards yet, I think it's okay. Plus this is a total emergency.

"Do you hear that guy, the one behind us, talking about how his drink is really, really weak and he wants to send it back and he doesn't have to gamble here and maybe he'll just take his business elsewhere?"

"The one who just screamed, 'Aces, baby, yeah!' like a tool?" Stuart asks happily.

"Yes," I say. "Could you . . . um . . . could you just . . . turn around and tell me what he looks like?"

Stuart, thankfully, doesn't ask questions. He just turns around and then back to me. "He has a goatee, short brown hair, and he's wearing a Celtics hat."

I close my eyes and sigh. "Thank you, Stuart."

"No problem."

"Um, one more thing," I say. "Can you let me know if he's looking over here?"

Stuart glances back. "Nope," he says.

I crane my neck back slowly and take a look. Yup. There he is, Leonardo, sitting with a big cup of something alcoholic, being loud and crazy and pretty much ruining my whole night with his presence.

I take a deep breath and start gathering up my chips. "Thanks, guys," I say. "But I gotta go."

No one protests, which kind of hurts my feelings, since I thought we were all friends. I rack up my chips and head over to Flo the cashier to turn them in. She hands me seven hundred-dollar bills, all crisp and perfect. It might be my imagination, or the fact that I'm in a better mood, but she seems a little friendlier this time.

"Thank you," I say, holding the bills in my hand and admiring their neatness. I resist the sudden urge to smell them. I'm definitely starting to understand how people can get so crazy about money.

I turn around and almost bang into Cole.

"Geez," I say. *"Stop doing that!"*

"What are you doing?" he asks. "Why did you get up?"

"Because my sister's boyfriend sat down at the table behind me, and I didn't want him to see me. It was probably good that I got up, anyway," I say. I shake the bills at him. "Because I won two hundred dollars."

He takes the money out of my hand and studies it. "Yeah, I know," he says. "I was watching you."

"You were?" I ask. "From where?" I look around behind me, wondering where he possibly could have been.

"It doesn't matter," he says. "We have to go, anyway. The Triple A guy called. The truck's almost here."

"Anyway," I say, following him as he starts to walk

out of the poker room, "did you notice that I was a natural? That I knew exactly what was going on, that I picked up on things like *that*?" I snap my fingers, in case he needs a visual of just how fast I was picking up on things.

"Yes," Cole agrees. "You did really well. You have some stuff to learn, but you did really great for your first night."

He's walking fast now, through the casino and toward the exit that leads to the elevator. I race to catch up with him.

"I know," I say. "I totally did. I won two hundred dollars! At a three-six table! On my first night, without any help whatsoever." It really is too bad that it's never going to happen again. I start to feel a little sad about that. I mean, this is definitely the easiest money I've ever made.

"I'm glad you had fun," Cole says. We're in the elevator now, and he pushes the button for the parking garage. The elevator starts to move, and he's looking up at the numbers, which are lighting up as we make our descent, and he looks almost . . . bored. My stomach flips.

Now that I've had a taste of this whole gambling thing, I kind of want to do it more. Uh-oh. Should I be worried? Yeah, it was fun. Yeah, I won two hundred dollars. But the fact that I changed my mind so quickly about gambling being shady, that it took only a little more than an hour for me to get high off winning and feel all jittery to do it again—it's kind of scary. Am I a gambling addict already?

And what's up with Cole's not saying anything about meeting up again? I mean, I *know* I can't do it again. Too risky. But you'd think he'd at least *ask* me if I wanted to. Is Aces Up kind of like a guy? Do I want them only because they don't want me?

The elevator doors open, and Cole saunters out ahead of me. Whatever happened to ladies first? My spirit slightly dented, I limp along behind him as he walks to his truck.

"Perfect timing," Cole says as the Triple A truck pulls up behind my car. Cole sits with me while the guy jumps my car. Once it's started, I wait for him to finally say something else about us meeting up again. But he doesn't. Instead, he just hands me two hundred-dollar bills from the stack I gave him. And then he gets in his truck and drives away.

The next day is Saturday, and when my alarm goes off at eight a.m., I'm already awake, lying in bed and thinking about the crazy happenings of last night. I slide out of bed, put on a pair of jeans and a soft green sweater, then brush my teeth and scrape my hair back into a ponytail. My plan is to get a super-early start on my homework for the week. And, um, do some catching up for last week. The house is quiet, but when I get downstairs, I find Leonardo sitting in our kitchen, eating a bowl of Honey Nut Cheerios and reading a magazine.

"Oh," I say. I did not expect to see Leonardo here. Of course, I didn't expect to see him at the casino last night, either. He's just popping up all over the place unexpectedly. Ugh. Okay, Shannon, I tell myself. Play it cool. Act natural. Think of what you'd say to him if it was any other morning. Probably something smart, so I force a cockiness into my tone and say, "I didn't know you could read."

"Oh, yeah," Leonardo says, obviously missing the sarcasm. "I love to read." He's wearing cargo pants and a brown T-shirt, and his leg is bouncing away under the table. Leonardo is always very . . . jittery.

"What are you doing up so early?" I ask. *Especially when you were out so late last night,* I want to add, but don't.

"Me and Robyn are going on a hike," he says. "But I'm not up early. I haven't been to bed yet." He looks at me expectantly. "I was out late last night, remember?" My heart starts beating super-fast, and I open the refrigerator and pull out the milk. I don't even want milk. But I need to do *something* to turn my back on him so that he can't see how red my face is.

"Um, no, I don't remember," I say, trying to keep my voice even. I put the milk on the counter and then realize that now I actually, you know, have to do something with it, so I pour myself a glass, then grab a Nutri-Grain bar out of the cupboard. Definitely time to take my breakfast to go. But *then* I realize that it would seem weird if I poured myself a glass of milk and left without drinking it, so I start gulping it down as fast as I can.

"But I saw you," Leonardo says. He takes a big slurpy spoon of cereal. "Last night." Ugh. *Stupid dumb Leonardo and his stupid dumb poker playing*.

"Um, no," I say, laughing. "I was working last night. Did you come into the Rusty Nail?" I arrange my features into what I hope is an innocent look. Nothing to see here, just everything being on the up-and-up, la la la.

"No," he says, frowning. "You were at the Collosio, right? I was there, too. At the poker tables." My heart starts pumping blood faster through my body, and I can hear a whooshing sound in my head. It feels like I'm panicking, so I take a long, deep breath and hope it doesn't show on my face.

"No," I say slowly and carefully. "I was at work. What would I be doing at the casino? I'm not even twenty-one!" I try to keep my voice light, like "Haha, isn't it funny you thought I was at the casino?" Of course, Leonardo's not twenty-one, either, but somehow it's not that much of a stretch to imagine him with a fake ID.

He frowns. "That's weird," he says. "I swear to God, it looked just like you. You were sitting at the poker tables, and it looked like you were having a good night." He puts his hands a few inches off the table to indicate a stack of chips. "You had a huge stack of chips."

"Yeah, well, I have a very common look," I say. "People are always thinking that they saw me out somewhere when they really didn't. In fact, just the other day, I was out and this girl on the street totally thought I was her cousin. Came up and hugged me and everything."

Leonardo frowns, his eyebrows knitting together. He pours himself some more cereal from the box on the table. "Really?" he asks.

"Totally." I take another sip of milk, forcing myself not to pour the rest of the glass down the sink. "And don't even get me started on the time this guy kept insisting I was the girl from camp he'd hooked up with two summers ago. Apparently she'd given him some kind of *disease,* it was completely—"

My dad chooses that moment to walk into the kitchen. He's whistling, but he stops when he sees Leonardo. "Oh," he says warily. "It's you."

"Hey, pops," Leonardo says. He gets up and pats my dad on the back. The weird thing about the whole Leonardo–my dad relationship is that Leonardo loooooooves my dad. He thinks he's the coolest cat around. (His words, obvi, not mine.)

"How did you get in here?" my dad asks. He shoots me a look, like he thinks I'm the one responsible, but I put my hands up in surrender and shrug as if to say, "Don't blame me, I would never let him in here."

"Robyn let me in," Leonardo says.

"And where is Robyn now?" my dad asks.

"She's upstairs, getting ready," Leonardo says. He pulls a mug down from the cupboard and busily pours a cup of coffee for my dad. "You need some coffee, pops." He says it as a command. Nice. Leonardo never offered *me* any coffee. All he did was tell me he saw me at the casino and try to ruin my life.

"Thanks," my dad says. He sets his laptop down on the table and boots it up. When my dad lost his job, we had to cancel our subscription to the newspaper, so now he gets all his news online.

There's a silence, and I panic, thinking maybe Leonardo is going to bring up the casino thing to my dad. "Robyn and Leonardo are going for a hike," I say quickly.

"Her idea," Leonardo says sadly. "Not mine."

"Yes, you know Robyn," I say. "Always trying to get you to go hiking with her!" I'm babbling now, so I pour the rest of the pot of coffee into one of my mom's Starbucks travel mugs. Definitely time for me to get out of here. And then my phone starts ringing in my pocket.

Who would be calling me this early?

I pull my phone out and check the screen. Ohmigod. It's Max! Max is calling me! The name Max is blinking right on my caller ID screen!

I don't know what to do. Answer, not answer. Answer, not answer. My finger flicks over the green button on my phone, back and forth, back and forth. If I answer, I'm going to be subjected to talking to him in front of my dad and Leonardo. If I *don't,* I'm going to wonder what he wanted.

And what if he doesn't leave a message? Then I won't know if I'm supposed to call him back. I mean, some people think that if you see a missed call from them, you should know you're supposed to call them back. But other people figure that if they don't leave a message, it doesn't necessitate a return phone call. Why didn't he just text me, like a normal person? Texting! Maybe I should text him. That would be okay, even if he didn't leave a message. Just a friendly text, saying—

"Are you going to answer that?" Leonardo asks. He takes another big spoonful of cereal. "That ringtone is driving me crazy."

Ugh. So I do. "Hello?" I say. Hmm. Maybe I should have said, "Hey, Max." Obviously he knows I know it's him because I looked at the caller ID. But maybe now he'll think I erased his number out of my phone. Do I want him to think that? Should I pretend I don't know who it is? Because then—

"Oh, hey," he says, sounding startled. "It's Max."

"Oh," I say. "Hey."

My sister comes running into the kitchen, wearing khaki shorts and a pink tank top.

"I'm ready!" she yells. "Ready to get my hike on!"

"I didn't think you'd answer," Max is saying. "I was going to leave a message."

"Then why did you call?" I ask, confused. Did he not want to talk to me? Was he hoping that I wouldn't answer, just so he could leave a message and not be subjected to having to deal with having an actual conversation with me? Are we going to be a tutor couple who does nothing but play phone tag? How. Lame.

"Uh, I wanted to set up a tutoring time," he says. I narrow my eyes and start to feel angry.

"Who are you talking to?" Robyn asks. She reaches past me and pulls a box of granola out of the cupboard. "Ugh," she says. "Who left the milk out? It's going to get all gross."

"You there?" Max asks. His voice sounds scratchy, like he just woke up. Very sexy. I picture him lying in bed, wearing only his boxers and a T-shirt. His face is scruffy, and his hair is all messed up. I imagine his body being all warm, and his shirt rides up a little bit as he reaches over to grab his phone off the nightstand to call me and . . . I take a deep breath. This is definitely not the way to stay mad at him.

"Yes," I say. "I'm here."

"So can you get together tonight?" he asks.

"Tonight?" I repeat.

"Yeah," he says. "Maybe around seven or so?"

Dilemma: admit I have no plans for Saturday night and tutor Max, or make something up so that I seem cool and alluring, but in return, give up the chance to hang out with him.

"I think that should work," I say. "I have nothing definite going on." "Nothing definite" is good. "Nothing definite" means I kind of sort of had plans but then

95

nothing was confirmed. How did I come up with that under pressure? God, I'm smooth.

"Who are you talking to?" Robyn asks again. At the table, my dad and Leonardo are having a heated discussion about the economy and the best way to fix it, and from what I can tell, Leonardo is, surprisingly, holding his own.

"So, um, seven at Barnes and Noble?" I say to Max. "I think that should take care of the deets." Oh, God. *Deets?* I've never used the word "deets" in my life. I heard Mackenzie say it to someone the other night, and I must have picked it up. How is that possible? That I heard something once and have now internalized it? My vocabulary has somehow turned into flypaper; apparently every crazy word is just sticking.

"Okay," Max says. "See you later, when you're more awake."

"What do you mean, when I'm more awake?" I'm perfectly awake. I'm about to start studying, for God's sake. I've already had a complete mini-drama, even, involving my sister's boyfriend and some illegal poker playing.

"Oh," Max says, sounding startled. "Nothing, I just . . . I mean, I figured you might have just woken up or something. Since it's so early. And, uh, because you sound kind of frantic."

"WHO ARE YOU TALKING TO?" Robyn practically screams.

96

"Call you later," I say to Max, and hang up before he can say anything else.

"Max," I say to Robyn. Just saying his name makes me blush, and Robyn's eyes widen. "I know," I say. "I'm tutoring him in math." I suddenly get very busy pouring cream and sugar into my coffee.

"You're *what?*" Robyn shrieks. My dad looks up from the computer, where he's pulling up some article to show Leonardo.

"I'm tutoring him," I say.

"Who's Max?" Leonardo asks, frowning.

"No one," I say firmly. "Just a guy I'm tutoring in math." I look Robyn right in the eye. "We're getting together tonight."

"He is *not* just a guy she's tutoring in math," Robyn reports. "He's this guy who totally broke her heart last year. He almost kissed her and then never called her again. He almost kissed and ditched!"

"That bastard," Leonardo says, which kind of makes me love him a little bit. But not enough to stop being mad at him for being at the casino. Which makes no sense, since *I* was the one doing something wrong, not him. This is all getting too complicated.

"Why didn't you tell me?" Robyn asks. She bites her lip and hops from one foot to the other, her ponytail bobbing. Unlike mine, Robyn's ponytail is perfectly smooth, except for one little flyaway that makes it look even cuter.

"I just found out," I say. "I'm sorry."

"It's okay," she says, and she squeezes my arm. "Are you cool with it, though?"

"Yeah," I say. "I'm totally cool with it."

"Don't worry," she whispers, leaning in close so that my dad and Leonardo won't hear. "We'll talk about it when I get home. And we'll figure out the perfect tutoring outfit."

I am such a horrible sister.

♥ ♠ ♣ ♦

Later that night. Barnes & Noble. I'm sitting in the café, waiting for Max to get back to our table with our drinks. My math book is open in front of me, and I'm trying to concentrate on some sample problems, but this is hard to do, since a) the fact that I am spending time with Max is making me extremely nervous, and b) there is an annoying kid in the corner who keeps screaming about this dumb ballet book she wants.

My sister, true to her word, spent more than an hour helping me find the perfect tutoring outfit: a light blue V-neck cotton sweater that shows just enough cleavage to be sexy but not enough that it looks like I'm dressed up, my best jeans, and a pair of Robyn's black boots with a heel. I have on lip gloss and two coats of mascara, and my hair is shiny and falls down my back, thanks to Robyn's diffuser and a deep-conditioning treatment (both her idea).

Fortunately, Robyn and Leonardo's hike took longer than it should have, so we didn't have too much time to get into the whole Max thing. And as far as I can tell, Leonardo never mentioned to her that he thought he saw me at the casino.

"Thanks," I say as Max returns to the table and hands me a steaming cup of coffee. He insisted on ordering drinks for both of us when he got here, which was pretty sweet. Still, this is awkward. I mean, how am I supposed to act? Are we going to have to have a big talk about what happened before we can start working? Will we just not talk about it? Do we have to keep things professional, talking just about math? Or will we talk about other things, too?

"No problem," Max says, and I take a sip. Ow. Hot. I resist the urge to spit coffee all over the table, and try to pretend like I haven't burnt my tongue.

"Um, how much was it?" I reach into my purse and pull out a couple of dollars, but Max waves me off.

"Don't worry about it," he says, and takes a sip of his own coffee. He's drinking it black, which I find very sexy. It's like he's strong and doesn't need to water down his coffee with sugar and cream. He can take it. I, on the hand, dump in about nine sugars and two tons of cream, which he totally remembered, because he made my coffee for me exactly how I like it.

"No, really," I say, shoving the money at him. "Take it."

"No way," Max says. "I'm not going to be that guy." Our hands touch as he pushes the money back at me, and my head feels all wobbly for a minute. Then I remind myself that even though he's being nice now, deep down he's a total jerk, and I should not fall for his supposed chivalry.

"What guy?" I ask.

"The guy who took two dollars from you for coffee."

"How do you know you'd be that guy?" I say, sliding the money back into my wallet and then sliding my wallet back into my bag. And furthermore, why would Max worry about being the guy who took two dollars from me for coffee, but not the one who totally blew me off after almost kissing me? I don't say this, though. In fact, I force my voice to sound light. "Maybe you'd just be the guy who I tutored, all the way back in my senior year." Or the one who blew me off after almost kissing me and never explained why.

He grins, his smile all crooked and cute, and I have the urge to reach across the table and run my finger over his lips. Bad, bad urge. I distract myself by blowing on my coffee, and a little bit of it flies up and into the air. Damn.

Why did I order boring old coffee? I should have ordered something like . . . I dunno, a chai tea. A vanilla chai tea. That sounds sophisticated and hip, like when Max and I stopped being friends, I changed my drink of choice from coffee to vanilla chai tea. Like *I'm* too cool for *him* now, and not the other way around. I wonder how much caffeine is in tea. However much is in this coffee is definitely not good for my nerves, because when my cell phone vibrates on the table with a new text message, I almost jump out of my chair.

It's from a number I don't recognize.

"It's Cole, did u get home ok last night?" it says, followed by a smiley. Hmmm. I've been trying not to think about Cole all day. I have come to the conclusion that what happened last night was a one-time thing, something I should most definitely *not* be getting involved in. I mean, I almost got caught by Leonardo. On my first night. I can only imagine how many other horrible things I might get into if I keep this up.

I know I shouldn't respond to the text. But for some inexplicable reason, I kind of want to. And Max is looking at me, and if I don't respond, he's going to think he's so important that I can just put my whole life on hold for him, which is definitely not the message I want to be sending.

"I'm fine," I text back. "And how did you get this number?"

"Anything important?" Max asks.

"Uh, no," I say, shutting my phone. "So should we get to work?" I need to think about numbers to keep my mind from thinking about . . . other things. Like Cole. And Max being so close.

"Okay," Max says. He hesitates and looks like he's about to say something, and then he leans over the table and lowers his voice. "But can I ask you something first?"

I swallow hard. "Sure," I say. I take another sip of my coffee and wish I'd gotten decaf.

Max leans in even closer, and I can see the little scar on the top of his lip, the one he got skateboarding when he was thirteen. "Look, I know this isn't any of my business," he says, "but why'd you need that fake ID and that birth certificate? Are you really a crazy gambler?" So much for the Chris Harmon School of Confidentiality.

"Oh," I say. I swallow hard, trying to move past the disappointment of his not bringing up what happened over the summer. "No, I just . . ." I'm about to make up an excuse, but my cell phone vibrates again.

"Got it from Mackenzie," Cole writes back. Ugh. Damn employee phone list. This time I decide not to reply.

"I just need them for something," I say lamely.

Max looks at me skeptically. Then he slides something out from between the pages of his math book and holds it up in front of me. My fake birth certificate! It looks real and perfect, my name typed neatly across the top. Although, if I'm reading it right, it looks like Chris Harmon decided my dad's name should be Mard Card. Which doesn't make much sense. But whatever! My fake birth certificate! But what is Max doing with it?

"Where did you get that?" I demand.

"From Chris," he says as I reach over the table and try to grab it from him. "Uh-uh," he says, pulling it out of my reach. "First you have to tell me why you need it."

I make another grab for it, this time almost toppling over the whole table. The girl in the corner who was so upset about her ballet book a couple of minutes ago looks at us and screams, "ROUGH-HOUSING IS NOT ALLOWED IN THE BOOKSTORE. MOMMY, THOSE TWO ARE ROUGHHOUSING!"

Max and I look at each other and burst into laughter.

And maybe it's kind of sort of because I want to tell somebody, or maybe it's because I felt so bad all day about lying to my sister, or maybe I just want to have a secret with him, to have some kind of connection back, or maybe it's just because I really do want that birth certificate, but the next thing I know, I blurt, "I got a job waitressing at the casino and you have to be twenty-one to work there, so I had to lie about my age."

Max looks shocked. He doesn't say anything for a minute, and at first I'm afraid that maybe he's going to get mad and give me some kind of huge lecture. But then he laughs, loudly enough that it echoes through the café and causes a couple of people to look. "That," he says, "is awesome." He slides the birth certificate across the table, and I pick it up and slip it into my purse.

"It is?" I ask, grinning. I decide not to tell him

about the other shady stuff that's been going on, as I'm sure he'd think that was decidedly less awesome.

"Yeah," he says. "I never would have guessed." His voice gets soft on that last part, and I'm not sure if I'm imagining it, but it seems like maybe he's sad he didn't know.

"Yeah, well," I say. I shrug. The lightness of the mood from just a second ago is gone, and I take another sip of my coffee to distract myself.

"I think it's cool you took matters into your own hands," he says. "I wish I could do something like that. I'm making, like, nothing at the gas station."

"You work at a gas station?" I ask. What gas station? Where? And how come I didn't know about this? Well, obviously it's because we're not friends anymore. And actually, it's probably a good thing I didn't know. Too much stalker temptation, as in I might be tempted to get gas there all the time. I take another sip of my coffee and try not to seem like I'm the kind of girl who would stalk someone at their place of employment.

"Yeah," he says. "The one on Holcum Road. Ever since my mom got laid off last month."

"Wow," I say. "I didn't know that." I've always liked Max's mom. She has crazy red curly hair, and every time I went over there, she was always offering me food. The cool thing was it was never cookies she had just baked or anything; it was always store-bought stuff, which was somehow better, like she wanted me to be comfortable at their house, but she wasn't putting on a front.

I wonder what Parvati thinks of Max's having to work at a gas station. I'll bet she doesn't like it. Unless she thinks it's like a movie, where she's sleeping with the pool boy or something, and everyone in her family will see Max's potential, and he'll end up rising to the top of her father's company, and they'll have a bunch of kids who will all have perfect teeth and perfect hair and get perfect scores in math. Ugh.

"So, um, anyway," I say, deciding that's enough secret sharing for now, mostly because it's making me feel really sad. "Maybe we should both work on the first three homework problems, and then we'll go over them. That way, I'll be able to see where you're having trouble."

"Sounds good," Max says.

I'm about halfway through the second problem (and Max is only about a third of the way through the first problem, uh-oh) when my cell starts ringing. My heart stops for a second, because at first I think it must be Cole calling to ask why I never responded to his text. But it isn't. It's Mackenzie. Adrienne made me program her number into my cell on my first night of work.

Why would Mackenzie be calling me? Unless she wants me to work tonight. Well, she can forget it. No way am I going to give up my tutoring session time with Max just to take a shift at work. Although I *do* need the money, I need to study, too. If my grades fall, I could lose my early-admission status with Wellesley.

"Are you going to answer that?" Max asks. He takes another sip of his black coffee. He doesn't even wince. Maybe he's used to it from all those early mornings at the gas station, when he has to rush out of bed and grab some strong coffee as soon as he gets there. Then he switches to water in the afternoon, after he gets all hot and sweaty from working on cars all day. And then he goes in the back and takes his shirt off so he can—

"Hello," Max says, picking my phone up off the table and handing it to me. "It's ringing."

"Oh!" I say. "Um, right. It's, uh, someone from work." I try to act like I wasn't answering it on purpose, not like I was distracted by my daydream in which Max morphed from Friendly Neighborhood Gas Station Attendant into Hot, Sexy Shirtless Mechanic. I send Mackenzie's call to voice mail, and five seconds later, I get a text. "I'M NOT GOING TO ASK YOU TO WORK," it says. "NOW PICK UP YOUR DAMN PHONE!!!" It immediately starts ringing again.

"Wow," Max says. "You might have a work stalker."

"Excuse me for just a second," I say. "Hello?"

"Finally!" Mackenzie screeches into my ear. "I've been trying to call you for *forever*."

"You've been trying to call me for two minutes," I say.

"Whatevs," Mackenzie says. "So, listen, we're going out tonight."

"Who's going out tonight?"

"Me and you," she says. "There's this party up at UConn, and I totally have to go."

"You want me to go with you to a college party?" I say incredulously. I can't just take off to a college party with her. I have to tutor Max. And besides, Mackenzie is the last person I want to go to a college party with. She's a little crazy. Then I remember that Mackenzie doesn't know I'm not in college, so I probably shouldn't have used the words "college party," because if I was in college, what other kind of party would I be going to? "I mean, you want me to go with you to a frat party?"

"Yes," she says. If she notices my slipup, she doesn't say anything. "I need to find out if Lance is going."

"Why don't you just call Lance, ask him if he's going to the party, and if he is, you can just meet him there?" Seriously, is she that dumb? I smile at Max apologetically and give him a look like "Crazy co-workers, what can you do?"

"Because," she says. "Lance is supposed to be study-ing tonight."

"So then why would he be at a party?" God, this is confusing.

"Don't you get it?" Mackenzie screeches.

"No," I say.

"Lance said he was going to be staying in, studying,"

she says. "But then I read on someone's Facebook page that there's a huge frat party tonight, and so I need to go."

"You want to go to the party to see if he's lying to you," I say as her horrible plan finally becomes clear.

"Yes!" she says. "And I want to see if that Facebook skank is there."

"What Facebook skank?" I ask.

Max raises his eyebrows at me.

"I'll pick you up in half an hour," Mackenzie says, ignoring my question.

"I can't," I say. "I'm, uh . . . I have plans."

"It's okay," Max says. "If you need to leave . . ."

"Who's that?" Mackenzie demands.

"That's Max," I say before I realize it might not be the best idea to tell her his name.

"Max who?" she demands.

"You don't know him."

"Well, he can come, too," she says. "You both can come. I'll pick you up, where do you live?"

"I'm in," Max says, slamming his book shut. Mackenzie's talking so loud he can hear her through the phone. "It's gotta be better than working on limits, right?"

Oh, Jesus.

♥ ♠ ♣ ♦

Two hours later, I'm sitting in the front seat of Mackenzie's car, worrying that this might just be the biggest mistake of my life. You know those *Dateline NBC* specials that are always on, about teens who end up in bad car accidents and/or get drunk at parties and have roofies slipped into their drinks? That's how this feels, like we're on our way to a place where, at any second, everything's about to go wrong.

"Don't you just love Big Gulps?" Mackenzie asks as we pull off the freeway. As soon as we got in the car, Mackenzie announced that we were stopping for gas and Big Gulps. She made Max and me both get one. A Big Gulp, I mean. I got Sprite, Max got Dr Pepper, and Mackenzie got Diet Coke. I guess I should be glad she didn't spike it with anything, but the caffeine is making her extra-hyper. Not me. The ice in my drink is all melted, making the soda taste watery, so I've mostly just been sliding my straw through it and wishing I was still drinking the coffee I had to abandon at Barnes & Noble.

The whole way to UConn, Mackenzie's been talking a mile a minute, mostly about Lance and some girl he's been talking to on Facebook. Apparently she found out about it by following some kind of photo tag trail. And now she has (of course) decided that Lance is a complete and total shit. She got Max on her side early. She'd say something like "And I think he's even been texting her on the side!" and Max would gasp and be all sympathetic. I feel like bringing up the fact that Max is just as much of a jerk as Lance, but that's something I don't really want to get into, much less in front of Mackenzie. Still. Talk about being a hypocrite.

"Don't you, Shannon?" Mackenzie presses as she turns the car onto a side road.

"Don't I what?" I ask warily.

"Love Big Gulps!" Mackenzie says like she can't believe I haven't been listening.

"I do love Big Gulps," I lie, because, you know, it's just easier that way.

We're pulling onto the UConn campus now, and Mackenzie is studying her GPS and looking at the houses, trying to find the best place to park. From the backseat, Max reaches out and tugs on my hair. I turn around, and he smiles at me. *Oh. My. God.* Max is pulling my hair! And smiling at me! It's almost enough to make up for the fact that I'm pretty positive that nothing good can come of this trip. But it also sets off a bunch of alarms in my head. Does Max think we're friends again? Do I want to be friends with Max again? Do I still like Max?

"Here we are," Mackenzie says, pulling over and sliding into a spot behind a Toyota Corolla with a Go Huskies bumper sticker. She pulls the rearview mirror down and checks her teeth for lipstick. "This," she declares, "is going to be crazy."

"Yeah," I say. "Totally crazy." I get out of the car reluctantly. "You know," I say, "it's not too late to change your mind about all this. I mean, Lance seems very trustworthy when it comes right down to it, doesn't he, Max?"

"Not really," Max says, getting out of the car and slamming his door. "I mean, didn't you hear what she said about how he used to turn his phone off late at night so that she couldn't get in touch with him? That doesn't sound too trustworthy to me."

Sigh.

"Yes," I say. "But that was before he got her those earrings from Tiffany, wasn't it, Mackenzie?" She's walking up the sidewalk now, toward the loud noise of the party, which we can hear coming from a couple of houses away.

"No," Mackenzie says. "That was *not* before he gave me those earrings from Tiffany." She sighs. "Geez, Shannon, weren't you even listening to the story?"

Not really. I mean, who could keep up with it? It was way too much information, and she kept going on and on and on and . . . *oops*. I'm walking a little too fast and I accidentally step on the backs of Mackenzie's shoes. "Sorry," I say. But she just waves me off and keeps walking. Wow. She's really on a mission. I'm actually a little bit scared of her.

My phone vibrates in my bag, and I flip it open. One new text.

"You up for playing again tomorrow, Shannon Card?" it says. Maybe I should sic Mackenzie on Cole. I flip my phone shut and slide it back into my bag, because I really can't deal with that right now, what with trying to keep up with everything that's going on here. Although prioritizing Mackenzie's drama with Lance and my own drama with Max over possible

111

illegal gambling dealings is probably not such a good idea.

We all troop up to the front of the house where the party's being held, and Mackenzie opens the door and walks right in. She makes her way through the sea of people hanging out on the staircase, sitting on couches in the living room, and playing beer pong in the kitchen. The air is thick with the smells of sweat and alcohol, and I follow Mackenzie, mostly because I don't know what else to do.

We do a lap around the house and finally end up on the back deck, where it's a little cooler and a lot less crowded.

"Did you see him?" Mackenzie asks anxiously. She stands up on her tiptoes and attempts to look through the double doors that lead back into the house. I don't know what she's looking for. All you can see is a bunch of shadows; it's too dim in there and we're too far away to be able to pick anyone out.

"Uh, no," I say truthfully. "I didn't see him." Which doesn't mean he's not here. It just means that I didn't see him. But I'm hoping Mackenzie will *think* he's not at the party and we can get the hell out of here.

"Did *you* see him?" she asks Max.

"I don't know what he looks like," Max says.

Mackenzie sighs, reaches into her bag, and pulls out her cell phone. She scrolls through her pictures and then shoves the screen in Max's face. "He looks like this," she says.

"Then, no, I haven't seen him," Max says seriously. I bite my lip and try not to laugh.

"Have you seen *her*?" Mackenzie asks, shoving the phone back at Max.

"Who's that?" Max asks, staring at the screen a little more closely.

"That," Mackenzie says, "is Ashley King, the skank who is after my boyfriend."

"You found out her name?" I ask in disbelief.

"You're damn right I did," Mackenzie says. She slides her phone back into her purse.

"How'd you do that?" I ask.

"Ashley King?" Max repeats. "She sounds like a porn star."

"She does sound like a porn star," Mackenzie says. She seems to like this. "A *skanky* porn star. And it wasn't that hard to figure out her name, Shannon, she was tagged in all the Facebook pictures." She pulls up the red tube top she's wearing, and her boobs threaten to spill out.

"Now you two stay here," she commands, "and I'll be right back."

She disappears into the house, leaving me and Max alone on the deck.

"So," I say to him once Mackenzie has cleared the area, "is this better than doing math problems?" Great. Real smooth. Realll great opening line, Shannon. Not that I'm trying to hit on him or anything. Because Max and I are just friends. Maybe not even friends. Maybe

113

just ex-friends. Maybe just teacher and student. In fact, we're not even *really* hanging out–he just happened to get dragged along on this crazy errand with me. And then I realize I must be a pretty horrible tutor. Taking my student out to a house party instead of tutoring him? Wellesley would definitely not approve of this.

"Much better than doing math," Max says. He sits down on one of the swinging wicker couches that are littering the deck, and then pats the seat next to him. I sit down, sinking into the scratchy turquoise cushion, and try to keep from obsessing about how close we're sitting.

"Where's Parvati tonight?" I ask. I can't resist. It's like I have to get the dig in.

"She went away for part of the weekend," he says. "With her family."

"Oh," I say. "Fun." We can hear the faint sound of music and the voices of people talking and laughing through the sliding glass doors. We just sit there for a little while, not saying anything, and every so often Max pushes his feet off the deck and we swing back and forth lazily. Now that we're not talking about math, I'm not sure what else to bring up. School? Lame. His job? Lame. That I'm secretly still in love with him and I don't know what happened to us and I miss him so much? Lame, lame, lame.

"You want a drink?" Max finally asks.

"Sure," I say, mostly because I'm desperate to do *something*. He disappears into the house and returns a minute later, holding two bottles of beer.

"Thanks," I say. My throat is suddenly super-dry, and I take a big gulp of the liquid, letting it run down my throat. I usually don't like beer, but I must be really thirsty, because this one tastes good, and I have to resist the urge to gulp it down. The last thing I need is to end up drunk. Not a good idea for a few reasons, not the least of which is that someone needs to keep an eye on Mackenzie.

"So do you think she's going to find him?" Max asks.

"Lance? I don't know."

Max leans all the way back and rests his head on the back of the swing. "What do you think she'll do?" he asks. "If she does find him, I mean?"

"I'm not sure," I say. "Probably something illegal."

His phone goes off then, and he reaches into his pocket, looks at the screen, and then slides it back in without answering. Was it Parvati? I take another sip of beer and tell myself I don't care.

"So tell me more about the casino," Max says. He turns toward me on the swing, and I lean back and turn toward him, too. I take another sip of my beer and close my eyes, letting the warm breeze wash over my skin.

"Nothing to tell," I say, shrugging. "I need the money for school."

"And you couldn't get a job waitressing at a restaurant, like a normal person?"

"It wouldn't be enough," I say. "Wellesley, remember? It's pretty expensive. Even with some loans and stuff, I'm going to have to make up the difference. And I got in early decision, so I don't really have a choice." My pointing out that he should remember where I want to go to school is the first time I've even remotely hinted at the fact that we used to be friends, that we used to know things about each other's lives. If he notices that, he doesn't react.

"The math award isn't going to be enough to cover it?"

"It's only five thousand dollars," I say. I'm suddenly very aware that we're alone out here. I mean, there are hundreds of people in the house, but out here? WE ARE ALL ALONE. ALONE. With no one around. It reminds me of the last time we were together, in the same situation, alone at a party and . . . I take another drink and push that night out of my thoughts.

"Sucks," Max says. "But it's okay, because you're going to be fine. You're going to go on to college, and then become some crazy-famous writer, and you'll make tons of money, and you'll look back on your time working at the casino and laugh about it."

"I will?"

"Totally."

"And will I use it in a book?" I ask him.

"Totally," he says again, smiling, and for a second, I think he's going to say something else. He looks almost wistful, but then his smile changes just a little and all he says is "You'll totally use it in a book."

We sit on the swing for the next forty-five minutes, catching up and talking about everything. School, our families, college. Everything except us and what happened over the summer and how we stopped being friends. I end up drinking two and a half beers, and I'm starting to feel all woozy and good, and that's probably one of the reasons I finally say, "So, what's the deal with you and Parvati?"

"What do you mean?" Max asks.

"Are you going to marry her?" I try to make my voice sound light, like I'm joking around, but Max frowns. He's wearing a navy blue sweater and I think about what it would be like to lay my head on his shoulder and bury my face in the softness of it.

"I'm only seventeen," he says.

"Almost eighteen," I remind him.

"Still," he says. "Way too young to get married. But don't tell Parvati that. She's been planning her wedding since she was five."

"Since she was *five*?" An image of a five-year-old Parvati collecting cutouts of wedding dresses with matching accessories passes through my head, and it's quite disturbing.

"Yeah." He takes another sip of his beer. "Don't all girls do that?"

Something about his lumping me into the same category as Parvati bothers me.

"I don't," I say, and it comes out more harshly than I intended.

"Well, you're different," he says. And there's something about the way he says it and the beer and the being outside alone and the breeze and the moon, and he's so close to me and I think about that night and wonder what would have happened if I'd called him after, if I'd done *something,* if I'd confronted him and told him how I felt, if maybe things would be different, and before I know it, I'm moving toward him and then we're really, *really* close and his lips are right there, and before I can stop it, I'm brushing my lips against his.

He looks shocked for a second, and his eyes widen, but then he brushes his lips against mine. I pull back, but then we're together again, kissing each other. *I. Am. Kissing. Max. Heller.* His lips are soft and perfectly moist, and his face is smooth against mine, and all of it is familiar and good and amazing, and the kiss goes on for what seems like maybe forever and at the same time maybe just a fraction of a second. Then he pulls away.

"Shannon," he says, and I know from the way he says my name that whatever he's about to say can't be good.

"I—" I start to say something about the alcohol messing with my head and, ohmigod, wasn't that funny and let's not tell anyone, hahahaha, but I'm still off balance from the kiss and the beer, and it's taking me a second to find the words.

And then Mackenzie comes flying out of the house

before I can say anything, her eyes wild and her blond hair a mess. "We have to get out of here," she says.

Max jumps up from the swing like he's on fire. Or like the swing's on fire. Or like *I'm* on fire. The point is he really wants to get away from me. "What happened?" he asks.

"Lots of things," I feel like saying but don't.

"They're here," Mackenzie says. She walks down the stairs of the deck and steps into the backyard, her heels sinking into the grass. "Lance and Ashley King." She says the name Ashley King the way you'd say "Angelina Jolie" or something, like she's just that famous. "And, uh, I kind of made a scene."

"What do you mean, you made a *scene*?" I ask, trying to keep up with her. Max is behind me, doing the same thing.

"Well, it wasn't a scene *exactly*," she says defensively. "It was really what any *normal* person would do when they found their boyfriend with another girl at a party."

"Like what?" Max asks. We've reached the front yard now, and Mackenzie looks up at the house nervously.

"Uh, we better hurry," she says. She reaches down and slips the straps of her shoes over her heels, then slides them off and into the huge purse she's holding. And then she starts to run. Max and I look at each other and then take off after her. But my shoes are still on, and even though they're not heels, like Mackenzie's, they're not exactly sneakers, either. So I slip and almost fall, but Max grabs me from behind.

"Thanks," I say, but I'm already taking his hands off my body. I don't need him to do me any favors, thank you very much. Whoa. I'm a little tipsy from the beers and the running, and I almost fall again, but this time I right myself immediately.

"Why are we running?" Max asks.

"Because," Mackenzie says. "I told you, I kind of made a scene."

We're at the car now, thank God, and I'm a little steadier on my feet. But not much.

"What did you *do*?" I ask, not sure I want to know. Although if she did something *really* bad, maybe it will make me feel better about kissing Max.

"I might have punched someone," Mackenzie says. She pushes the button on her key chain, and the car beeps as the automatic locks unlock.

We all climb in.

"You might have *what*?" I ask as I hold the passenger seat forward so that Max can climb into the backseat. I try to give him a smirk as he passes, one of those "That's right, buddy, you're in the backseat" kind of expressions, but he's not even looking at me.

"Oh, relax," Mackenzie says as she puts her seat belt on. "It was barely even anything. In fact, it was more of a graze."

"Oh, God," I moan, leaning my head back against the seat. "Why did you do that?"

"Because," Mackenzie says, pulling onto the highway. I hope she's not going to get all worked up and start driving all crazy. Her Big Gulp–induced caffeine high was way better than this. Thank goodness she hasn't been drinking. At least, I don't think she has.

"Have you been drinking?" I ask.

"When would I have had time to have a drink?" she asks. "I've been running around all night, trying to catch my boyfriend in an act of infidelity! Besides, I couldn't do what I did with my faculties compromised." She grips the steering wheel tightly and looks at me closely. "Why, have you?"

"Have I what?"

"Been drinking."

"A little," I admit.

"Oh, great," she says. "I'm having a huge personal crisis, and you're out getting drunk."

"She's not drunk," Max pipes up from the backseat.

"How do you know?" I ask. How annoying. That he thinks he knows if I'm drunk. I mean, *obviously* I must be. I would never have kissed him if I wasn't *obviously* out of my mind, drunk and crazed.

"You only had two beers," he says.

"Two and a *half*," I say. "And they were *bottles*. And I'm a lightweight. I'm definitely drunk. In fact, I've never been this drunk!" It's not true, but as I say it, I almost start to believe it. My head definitely feels all wobbly, and my heart is beating fast, and my face feels flushed.

"Well, that's just fabulous," Mackenzie says, sounding annoyed. "You'd better not get sick in my car."

"I won't," I say. "If you want to worry about anyone getting sick, you should worry about Max back there."

This doesn't really make sense, but Max gets the message. The message being, you know, to shut up. And Mackenzie must get it, too, because everyone is quiet the rest of the ride back. Mackenzie drops me off first, since Max lives closer to her.

"Bye," I say, slamming the car door and running up the sidewalk, because that's the only thing left to do.

On Monday morning, I wake up with a splitting headache, and I'm so not looking forward to going to school. Especially since Max did not call me or attempt to reach me at all on Sunday. I spent the whole day trying to catch up on my homework and, of course, obsessing over my phone. I also made a playlist for my iPod called Boys Suck. It's a compilation of tons of girl rock, everything from Christina Aguilera to Tori Amos. (Not that I have Tori Amos on my computer. I'm not cool enough. But Robyn has a lot of it, and we have shared libraries.)

I figured Max would at least want to talk about it. The whole kiss thing. Or non-kiss. Or kiss that started out as a kiss and turned into a push-away. I mean, he knows we're going to see each other at school. Does he not want to get any potential awkwardness out of the way?

Apparently not, since, like I said, he didn't call. Finally, on Sunday night, I had to take my cell phone out to my car and lock it in the trunk. Which is unfortunate, since it seems to be slightly frozen now, and some of the keys are sticking together.

Anyway, now it's Monday, and even though I'm super-tired and my head is pounding (the two Excedrin I downed apparently having no effect), I am at school. Not only that, but I am here half an hour early. This is because I have decided I'm not going to take any of this lying down. So what if Max didn't call me? I have much more important things to do—for example, asking Ms. Kellogg about doing some extra credit so that I can keep my transcript in tip-top shape for Wellesley. I am way too busy and important to worry about some dumb boy and his dumb, stupid not calling me.

When I get to the math wing, I can see Ms. Kellogg through the strip of glass in the door. She's at her desk, sipping from a mug and looking at some papers. I knock, and it's only when she motions me in that I realize I've just walked into my worst nightmare.

Max is sitting at one of the desks near the front of the room, working on what looks like a makeup test. And as if this isn't enough of a complete and total travesty, Parvati is sitting near the front of the room, too, a bunch of papers spread out all over her desk.

"Oh," I say, surveying the scene and already trying to figure out a way to get out of there. "Um, I can come back."

"No, no, it's okay," Ms. Kellogg says.

"Hi, Shannon," Parvati says, breaking out into a huge smile. She looks very Parvati-like today, in a light blue skirt, a lacy white blouse, and blue and white patent leather wedges, which is even more annoying to me than usual. Of course, my annoyance probably has less to do with her outfit and more to do with the fact that less than forty-eight hours ago, my lips were on her boyfriend's.

"Hi," I say warily, not making eye contact with her. Does she know I kissed Max? Does she know that he kind of sort of kissed me back? Did Max tell her about the push-away? Does she want to fight me? Could I take her in my compromised state? Although if she knew anything about what happened on Saturday, she probably wouldn't be acting so happy to see me.

I look at Max for some kind of clue, but he keeps his eyes on his test and doesn't say anything.

"What's up?" Ms. Kellogg asks. She looks like she could be Parvati's older sister, in a pink lace shirt, a pink and cream skirt, and pink pumps with a cream stripe. Ugh.

"Um, I just . . . I was wondering if there's any extra credit I could do besides tutoring," I say. "I'm really trying to keep my grades up for Wellesley."

Ms. Kellogg and Parvati look at each other and burst out laughing. Geez. Talk about adding insult to injury.

"What's so funny?" I ask.

"I was just here about Wellesley, too," Parvati says. "I was asking Ms. Kellogg if she would write me a recommendation." She picks up one of the papers on her desk and waves it in the air. Across the top it says "Form for Undergraduate Admission."

Oh. I didn't know Parvati wanted to go to Wellesley. "I didn't know you wanted to go to Wellesley," I say. I have a vision of getting my "Welcome to Wellesley, and your roommate is" letter in the mail, with Parvati's name in it. That would be awkward. What would we do when Max came to visit for the weekend? Not to mention that Parvati might be, you know, the most annoying girl on the planet. Plus we'd definitely need a big room so she could fit all her shoes.

"I don't, really," she says. "What I really want is Harvard." Her eyes glisten as she says "Harvard," like she can't even contain her excitement. "But Max told me at dinner last night he's thinking about Boston College, and so I just figured I should have a backup nearby, you know?" She bites her lip and looks thoughtful.

I narrow my eyes and glare at Max, even though he's staring intently at his paper. Apparently while I was having to resort to stashing my cell phone in my trunk, Max was out with Parvati, romancing her at a restaurant and planning their futures. I feel tears prick a little bit at my eyes, but honestly, what did I expect? Max blew me off once; why would I think he wouldn't do it again?

"Anyway, this is so coooolll," Parvati says. "We can totally do Wellesley extra credit together!" The way she says it is like "We know I won't need it as much as you do, but let's both pretend."

"So exciting!" Ms. Kellogg says. "My two best students, maybe ending up at the same college!"

"Yeah, maybe," I say. Max is still bent over his paper, not saying anything.

"Well, I should go," Parvati says. "I have to be at the yearbook office." She gathers up all her papers, then gives Max a kiss on the cheek and disappears out the door in a cloud of expensive-smelling perfume.

"So," Ms. Kellogg says once Parvati is gone, "you can most certainly do some extra credit. Let's try to figure something out, shall we?" We spend a couple of minutes going over some of the possibilities, and then, thank God, I'm out of there. It was totally uncomfortable with Max being in the room the whole time.

I feel a little better once I leave the classroom, but when I'm a few feet down the hall, I hear someone calling after me. Max. I just keep going, my eyes trained ahead. I square my shoulders and pretend I'm Rosa Parks or Gloria Steinem or some other important and honorable woman who doesn't take any crap from guys or anyone else. Which is completely over-dramatic, I know, but kind of helps me feel better.

"Shannon," he says when he finally catches up to me. "Listen, I'm sorry about that. I didn't want to say anything in front of . . . I mean, we should prob-ably . . ."

"No," I say. "We probably *shouldn't*." I pick up my pace, my footsteps echoing angrily down the empty hallway.

"Shannon!" he says, running after me and then stepping in front of me, blocking my way.

"What?" I say, crossing my arms over my chest.

"I don't know," he says. "I . . . I want to talk about what happened." He moves the books he's holding from one hand to the other and looks at me intently.

"Oh," I say, laughing incredulously. "*Now* you want to talk about what happened?" It's like all the anger from the past few months is bubbling over, and before I know it, I'm letting it out. "You mean what happened this weekend? When you kissed me back even though you had a girlfriend? Or what happened over the sum-mer? When you *didn't* kiss me and then stopped being my friend?"

I'm yelling now, and Max looks kind of shocked. Probably because I've never mentioned any of this be-fore, and also because I'm not the kind of girl who goes crazy and has hallway confrontations. Well, until now, apparently.

"Shannon," Max says. He looks nervous. "Look, can we . . . maybe after school we could talk, we could . . ."

"If you wanted to talk so bad," I say, "then why didn't you call me yesterday?"

"I wanted to," he says. "I did. I just . . ." And for a second, I think that if he tells me he was with Parvati, if he tells me that it's complicated but that he still wants to talk about it, then maybe, just maybe, I'll say yes. Because at least I'll know he's being honest with me. And everything seems to stand still for a second, but then all he says is "I just . . . didn't."

So I turn and walk away. He calls my name, but I ignore him, and he doesn't come after me, so I just keep going. Because honestly, what do we have left to talk about? How I humiliated myself the other night? How he's in love with Parvati? How he probably doesn't think it's a good idea for me to tutor him anymore? How I was so *stupid* to think we could be friends again? How I should have listened to my instincts, and my sister (who, by the way, is *always* right about these things), and never started to tutor him in the first place? I mean, hello! How stupid can I be?

So I just keep walking. And with every step, I get sicker and sicker of everything. Sick of being the one who has to be let down easily by the guy she likes. Sick of being the one who has to lie to her parents and work her ass off just to make a hundred dollars a week. Sick of being the one who can't go to her dream school because of money.

And almost before I even realize what I'm doing, I reach into my bag and pull out my cell. I scroll through the text messages until I get to the one I'm looking for, and then I type in a text to Cole.

"Hey," I say. "I want to play tonight. You in?"

♥ ♠ ♣ ♦

When I get home from school, there's a man standing in our driveway. He's about my dad's age, has short dark hair, and is wearing khaki shorts and a blue sweater. For a second, I'm afraid to get out of the car, because a) ever since I started breaking the law, I am totally suspicious of strange men, and b) the last time I came home to find a guy in our driveway (aka Butch), it wasn't good news.

"Oh, hello," the man says to me, his tan face happy and shiny.

"Hi," I say warily. "Um, can I help you?"

"Yes," the man says. "I–"

My dad comes bustling out of the house. "So sorry, so sorry!" he says. "You must be Fred. I'm David Card. I see you've met my daughter Shannon."

I can tell from the way my dad is acting that this isn't the time to ask questions, so I just say, "Okay, I'll leave you to it," and head inside. Maybe it's a job interview! Like a home visit when they get to the second round or something.

"Who's that guy out there with Dad?" I ask Robyn when I get inside. She's sitting at the kitchen table, eating a huge piece of cake with vanilla frosting and looking through a bunch of papers. I drop my bag onto a chair and glance at the clock over the microwave. I have about twenty minutes before I leave for work, and that includes time to shower.

"He came to see about the boat," Robyn says.

"The boat?" I frown. "Oh, is he taking it to be stored for the season?" My dad has a boat. Just a small one, which he used his bonus from a few years ago to buy. Right now it's just sitting in our garage, though, because he couldn't afford to take it out this summer. My mom's been bugging him to get it stored somewhere before the winter gets here.

"No," Robyn says. "Dad's selling it." She hands me a piece of paper off the table.

It's a digital printout showing our boat along with all the specifics, like how big it is and how much he wants for it. "He put it online this morning and apparently he already has interest."

"He's *selling* the boat?" I ask incredulously. The boat is like my dad's . . . I don't know. The car is one thing. But the *boat* . . . In the summer, on the weekends, you can't get him off the thing. We have a lot of really great family memories involving that boat. He loves that boat. "But he loves that boat!" I say.

"Yeah," Robyn says. She sighs. "But Hank Blumenthal was let go today from Farber Bank."

Great. Hank Blumenthal hooking him up was pretty much my dad's best shot at a new job. God, can this day get any worse? I open the refrigerator door and scan the contents before deciding to follow Robyn's lead and go for the cake. I feel like I've earned it after the day I've had. I cut myself a huge hunk, pour a big glass of milk, and sit down at the table, ready to wallow.

"And what are you doing?" I ask Robyn. I shovel a big spoonful of cake into my mouth and delight in the sugary icing.

"Scholarship applications," she says. "Otherwise I don't know how we're even going to pay for community college next semester."

After that I'm too depressed to eat. I consider dumping my whole plate of cake into the garbage, but then realize that it would be a total waste of money, so instead, I wrap it up in plastic wrap for later.

Then I drag myself upstairs and into the shower. While I'm in there, the warm water sliding over my body, my cell phone rings. My heart jumps into my throat for a second, and I reach out and grope around on the bathroom floor and in the pocket of my jeans, where my phone is. It might be Max. But it isn't. It's Cole.

"Hello," I say. He never replied to my text today, which is fine with me. I mean, I *obviously* sent it in a moment of insanity and craziness. I do not want to play poker again. I do not even want to *think* about poker again. I was just upset about a guy, nothing more. Well, maybe a little more. Like I might have been having a complete and total meltdown.

"So you want to play tonight, huh?" Cole asks. From what I can hear in the background, it sounds like he's already at the casino. I hold the phone against my shoulder and try to keep it from getting wet.

"Ignore that text," I say. "I wasn't thinking." The shampoo bottle falls into the tub, so I bend down and grab it.

"Really?" His tone is dark and serious, and suddenly, I don't know if I mean it. I mean, there's nothing really wrong with it, right? Gambling? If you do it at the casino, it's totally legal. And yeah, I'm underage, but not by that much.

And besides, isn't gambling pretty much what everyone at my dad's company was doing? The whole financial system is kind of a big gamble—gambling on people to be able to make their payments, gambling on the stock market and hoping you'll make money, gambling with your investments and hoping you're putting your assets in the right places.

"Yes, really," I say. But I sound less sure this time. I watch some of the soapy water circle around the drain. "I don't want to gamble."

"Poker isn't gambling," he says. "It's a skill-based game. And if you didn't want to play, then why did you send me that text?"

"I had a bad morning," I say.

"Are you in the shower?" he asks.

"No," I lie.

"Then what's all the water noise?"

"I don't know what you're talking about," I say. I spin around and rinse my hair off quickly, then turn off the water.

"Whatever," he says. "So I won't see you tonight?" I hesitate for a second. I think of my dad outside, trying to convince a stranger to buy his boat; my sister at the table in the kitchen, filling out scholarship applications; and my mom at work, picking up an extra shift to help out with the bills.

"How much could I win?" I ask. "I mean, uh, just out of curiosity?"

"How much do you want?" he asks in that annoyingly cocky way of his.

"A hundred thousand." I'm trying to shock him, but he doesn't sound shocked. He just laughs like I'm a little child who's been told she can have anything in the candy store and has chosen a Dum Dum lollipop.

"Oh, Shannon Card," he says, "am I going to have fun with you."

I lean my head against the tile and think for a second. "Okay," I say, deciding. "I'll meet you after I get off work at ten."

"Cool," he says. "I'll be in my hotel room. And make sure you wear something sexy." At first, I'm sure I've misheard him. Wear something *sexy*? Who says that?

"*Excuse me?*" I say, incredulous. "I will not dress sexy just so that you can . . . get your rocks off."

"Get my rocks off?" Cole sounds amused. I grab my towel off the rack and wrap myself in it, then step out of the shower.

"Yes," I say. "You know what getting your rocks off means, don't you?"

"Oh, I know what it means," he says. "That's why I was laughing."

"Ugh," I say. "You know what? I really don't–"

"Look," he says, "it's not for me. I don't care what you wear. But it might be better to wear something a little revealing."

"Because?"

"Because if you can play into the whole 'I'm a girl and I don't know anything about poker' thing, you have a better chance of taking money from the other players."

Oh. Well. Part of me is definitely offended. Showing off my boobs so that I can get more money? What is up with everyone lately? Mackenzie urging me to wear a push-up bra, Cole trying to get me to wear something revealing so that guys will think I'm stupid? But another part of me is thinking that if guys want to underestimate me, why shouldn't I do anything I can to maximize my chances? It's like how my dad would always wait for a company to release its earnings reports, and if they were good, of course he'd buy the stock. You do what you can to give yourself the best odds.

"Fine," I say. "I'll meet you at ten o'clock." I hang up the phone and get ready to raid Robyn's closet for something appropriately revealing.

♥ ♠ ♣ ♦

When I get to work, I realize quickly that Mackenzie is not in a good mood.

"Hello!" she says as soon as I walk into the lounge. "Thanks for calling me yesterday!" She crosses her arms over her chest and taps her shoe on the carpet, her eyes accusing.

I frown. "I'm sorry," I say. "Did we have plans?" I rack my brain, trying to remember. I was so out of sorts because of the Max thing on Saturday night that I don't remember much about the conversation (or lack thereof) that took place on the way home. It's totally possible that Mackenzie tried to make a plan and I forgot about it. But if she did and I didn't show up, then why didn't she call or text me? "Did you try to call?" I ask. "I had to put my phone in the trunk, and it got frozen."

Her mouth drops open. *"Plans?"* she asks. "No, we did not have *plans*. We *should* have had plans, you should have been taking me out to breakfast or brunch or out to a *bar* or something, helping me *repair* my broken heart." She sniffs. "I had to spend the whole day watching *Project Runway* by myself."

"Oh," I say, still not getting it. "I'm sorry, I really didn't know we had plans."

"Shannon," she says. She grabs me by the shoulder and looks into my eyes. "We. Did. Not. Have. Plans. But you could have called to check on me. That's what *friends* do."

"Oh," I repeat. Um, I didn't know Mackenzie and I were friends. Otherwise I would have been happy to call her. Maybe not to take her out to a bar (apparently drinking is not good for me), but definitely brunch. I could have totally used some brunch yesterday, maybe eggs Benedict and French toast with lots of syrup. "I didn't know we were friends," I try.

"Of course we are!" she says. "Why do you think I invited you to come with me to see if Lance was cheating on me?"

"Because you didn't have anyone else to go with?" I ask. I move past her to my locker in the corner and shove my bag in. My shoes fall out and clatter to the floor, and I pick them up and shove them back in. They really need to get bigger lockers around here. You'd think that with all the money they're making every night, they could afford to treat their employees a little better.

"Well," Mackenzie says, "that *is* true. That I didn't have anyone else to go with. But I still wanted to go with you. I mean, I *could* have gone by myself."

"Okay," I say. "So we're friends. Thanks for clearing it up, and next time, I will be sure to take you to brunch. My treat, even." Why not? I mean, I'm about to be rich, right?

"Shannon," Mackenzie scolds, "now that we're BFFs, we're supposed to support each other, especially when it comes to guys."

Hmmm. "Don't you already have a BFF?" I ask.

"No," she says, sighing. "You'd think that I would, but honestly, most girls don't like me." Surprise, surprise.

"Look, you don't need Lance," I say, trying to make up for my lack of support yesterday. Better late than never, right? "You're way better than Lance, with his dumb tattoos and his dumb wallet chains! I mean, how 1999 can you get?" Hopefully they don't get back together. I could never hang out with Lance again after all this bad-mouthing. Too embarrassing.

"Really?" Mackenzie perks up a little.

"Totally," I say. "I mean, you have tons of guys hitting on you every night. You could have any guy you wanted. Lance is going to rue the day he ever broke up with you for that ridiculous . . ." I search for a term Mackenzie would love to hear applied to Ashley King, and settle on "skank whore." It rolls off my tongue surprisingly well.

"Well," Mackenzie says, cocking her head to the side and thinking about it, "I *did* meet a guy at the party before I found Lance upstairs with the skank whore."

"You did?" I ask, pleased that she's deemed my term worthy enough to add to her vocabulary.

"Yes," she says. "What did you think was taking me so long?"

"I wasn't sure," I say truthfully, not mentioning that I really didn't care since I was enjoying having Max all to myself.

"Anyway, his name is Filipe, and he seems really

nice." She wrinkles her little nose. "Definitely not a cheater. We've been texting all day."

"There you go!" I say. "See? You're already back in the game!"

Mackenzie grabs me in a hug. "Thanks, Shannon."

"You're welcome," I say into her hair.

♥ ♠ ♣ ♦

Work. Goes. By. So. Very. Slowly. I'm completely scattered and unfocused. I spill two drinks and forget to add the alcohol to one of the players' Diet Cokes. And he is not happy. At all. ("How could you forget the rum? The rum is what keeps me going! Where's a comment card? I think I need to fill out a comment card!")

But by the time my shift is over, I don't even care that my feet are killing me and that Adrienne has been on my back all night. ("Move it, Shannon, this isn't an old-age home!" "Shannon, my grandma could move better than you!" "Shannon, where are the drinks for table eleven!") Honestly, it's verging on verbal abuse. Plus when I gave her my fake birth certificate, she acted like she didn't even care, like she hadn't been practically *hounding* me for it. But like I said, I don't even care. I'm too nervous about the fact that I'm going to be back out at the tables soon.

"I'm going out with Filipe tonight," Mackenzie offers up when we're in the dressing room after our shift. "He texted and asked me if I wanted to have a late dinner."

"Really?" I say. "That's great."

I open my bag and survey its contents.

Here's what I packed:

- red dress of Robyn's that is too big for her, so it
    might fit me
- tight black pants
- tight white T-shirt
- black dress with flippy skirt, also taken from
    Robyn's closet, also too big for her
- curling iron
- straightening iron (Obviously I can't decide how
    I want to wear my hair.)
- black boots
- everything I could find in my makeup drawer

I look at the mess and contemplate whether I should just change back into my jeans and pink hoodie. I know Cole said to dress sexy, but that can't *really* make any difference, can it? It's going to depend on how well I play, not what I look like. I've decided I don't want to win because guys are underestimating me, anyway. I want to win on my own merits. With my own skills. Plus won't it look weird if I end up out on the floor all dressed up and ready to play? What will the people I work with think? Then again, they probably won't even notice, since no other waitress besides Mackenzie has ever spoken to me, and when I played the other night, the pit boss didn't even recognize me. Sigh.

140

And then a picture of Parvati flashes through my mind, and she's at Wellesley, talking with a bunch of girls, and they're all deciding which literary society to join (because you just know she's that type), and Max is up for the weekend and she's so happy to see him, and I'm weaving through the tables at the Collosio, still working here so that I can make money for gas to get me back and forth to the community college. And so I decide I need any advantage I can get.

"So then I said, 'Well, I've never been to that restaurant,' and then he said, 'Well, a beautiful girl like you definitely needs to go there.' Isn't that so sweet?" I realize that Mackenzie has been talking to me this whole time, her voice coming over the door to the private dressing area I'm standing in. I haven't heard a word. I really need to do a better job of being a good BFF.

"That's really sweet," I say, opening the door. "Listen, Mackenzie," I say. "I need some advice."

Mackenzie gets a serious look on her face, grabs my shoulders, pushes me over to the little sitting area in the corner, and plops me down in a chair. "Is it about Max?" she asks. "Spill."

"Uh, no," I say. "It's not about Max."

"Oh." Mackenzie's face falls. "Then what is it about?"

"Um, well, it's kind of about fashion," I say. I open my bag and show her the contents. "If you wanted to be, uh, sexy and revealing, what would you wear out of this stuff?"

Mackenzie surveys the contents closely and frowns. "Shannon, you really shouldn't treat your clothes like this. If you leave them all bunched up, they're going to—OHMIGOD, YOU HAVE PRADA BOOTS!" She screams and holds them up. Then she kicks off the shoes she's wearing, a pair of silvery heels, and shoves her feet into the boots. "Where did you get these?"

"Christmas present from my aunt," I say. "And they're not real. They're knockoffs."

"Oh." Mackenzie's face falls again, and she pulls off the boots.

"They're still good," I say defensively. "You couldn't even tell they were fake."

"Of course they're still good," Mackenzie says soothingly, and pats my head.

I sigh. I'd better not have to dress revealingly forever. Just until I become a kick-ass poker player and people know not to mess with me. "So, uh, what do you think about this stuff?"

She surveys my belongings. "Well," she says, "I'd wear this"—she holds up the black dress—"with the boots, of course. And you should blow your hair straight with a round brush to give it volume at the bottom, and then some smudged eyes with a nude lip."

She lost me with the nude lip. "Okaaay," I say slowly. "But what if I needed to, you know, get into this stuff now, and I didn't have any round brushes or nude lips?"

"Then you'd borrow it from me," she says, frowning.

"I keep all that stuff in my locker for when I go out after wo— Wait a minute! Shannon! Where are you going this late and why are you getting all vamped up?"

"Vamped up? I'm not getting vamped up, I'm just trying to—"

"You *are* going out with him, aren't you?" she says. She leans across the table and she's so close to me I can see the sparkles on her cheeks that have flecked off from her eye shadow.

"Who?" Please don't say Cole, please don't say Cole, please don't—

"Max!" She sighs. "Shannon, I'm a little upset that you haven't told me."

"Oh, no," I say. I'm so relieved she doesn't know I'm hanging out with Cole that I almost don't even mind that she brought up Max's name. "I told you, we're just friends. I'm, um . . . I'm going out with another guy."

"Ooh," she says. "We both have fun nights planned, just the way we should." She nods. "I'll help you get ready." I follow her obediently to the side of the room, where she reaches into her bag and pulls out a pair of black stockings. "You," she declares, "are going to look hot as hell. Now, tell me all about this guy."

♥ ♠ ♣ ♦

Twenty minutes later, I realize that Mackenzie's right. I do look hot as hell. I'm wearing Robyn's black dress (which is a little tight on me, but in a good way, because it shows a lot of cleavage and looks like it's tight on purpose), a pair of black patterned stockings, and the fake Prada boots. My hair is free and flowing around my shoulders, and my eyes are smoky and smudged with some gray and black eye shadow of Mackenzie's, along with three coats of black mascara. My lips are covered with a light pink gloss, making my eyes pop even more, and Mackenzie dusted my shoulders with some sheer sparkling powder, and my face with some bronzer. I've never looked so good in my life.

"You," Mackenzie says, "are going to totally wow this guy, whoever he is." She gives me a kiss on the cheek. "Have fun," she says. "Text me if you need anything."

She's nice, I think as I walk out of the dressing room. I make a mental note to text her later and ask her how her date went. And then I head to the side of the casino and take the elevator up to room 2123.

8

$\mathcal{I}$knock on the door to Cole's room. Nothing. I knock again. Still nothing. Is there some sort of secret knock? Or a password I'm supposed to shout out? I try beating a little rhythm on the door, one knock, then wait, two knocks, then wait. Still nothing.

I'm debating whether I should call him on my cell to figure out what's going on when the door finally swings open and Cole's standing there wearing a towel. A TOWEL. Around his waist. And nothing else.

He's . . . very built. He has a six-pack. I try to avert my eyes, but it's hard.

"What took you so long?" I ask haughtily, trying to pretend it's every day that a half-naked guy opens his hotel room door for me.

"Sorry," he says. "I was in the shower." Obviously. He looks me up and down, and suddenly, my sexy outfit, which seemed like a good idea back in the dressing room, seems silly. What was I thinking? This isn't me. I'm not *sexy*. I wear jeans and hoodies or maybe a V-neck sweater if I'm feeling daring.

Cole leans in close to me. "You look really hot," he whispers. His breath is warm on my ear, and it smells like something dark and sweet. Maybe rum. My first inclination is to pull away, because his nearness is making me feel a little weak, but instead, I just say, "Thanks," and push past him into the room.

My stomach does a flip, and the old familiar feeling of being in a weird place with a sketchy guy I hardly know washes over me. I take a deep breath. It's okay, I tell myself. If he wanted to kill and/or maim you, he's already had tons of chances to do it.

Cole goes into the bathroom and reappears a few minutes later, wearing a pair of jeans and a black T-shirt. His hair is still wet, and it flops onto his forehead.

"So," he says. He sits down at the table in the room and motions to the seat across from him, and I sit down. "Are you really in?"

"What do you mean?" I ask, suddenly nervous.

"I mean," he says, "that you can't just pop up every

time you feel like being a badass, or when you need a little extra money. You're either in or you're out."

"I'm here, aren't I?" I say, trying to sound surer than I feel. I mean, this is kind of serious. Deciding to join a secret poker society? Major.

"So I convinced you," Cole says. He breaks into a huge grin.

"You didn't *convince* me," I say. "I decided it all on my own." Which is true. He didn't convince me to do anything. In fact, if anything, he's pushed me *not* to join, by acting all shady.

"Because of me convincing you."

"Nooo," I say. "Because of me deciding all on my own." The way he's looking at me is making me uncomfortable, so I pull my eyes away from his gaze and focus on the wall behind him.

"Then, what happened?"

"What do you mean?"

"Usually when people say no to joining Aces Up and then decide they want to, it's because something in their circumstances has changed."

"Nothing in my circumstances has changed," I say. It isn't technically a lie. Just because I found out that Parvati wants to go to Wellesley and I tried to kiss Max and he didn't respond and my dad is now consumed with selling off all our possessions, it doesn't mean my circumstances have changed. I mean, I'm still working at the casino. I have the exact same financial situation as I did before.

"You don't have to tell me." Cole shrugs and

reaches for a deck of cards sitting on the table. He starts shuffling them fast, back and forth from hand to hand.

"I told you, there's nothing to tell," I say.

He shrugs again. "I don't really care either way." Shuffle, shuffle. "You know, usually we don't let people in who have said no first," he says. "But we like you."

"Thanks," I say. "Who is this 'we' you keep talking about, anyway? Like, where is everyone else?" I kind of expected that there'd be group meetings. You know, PowerPoint presentations, maybe dinners out . . . like in that movie *21*.

"They're around," he says. "But you'll mostly be dealing with me." He's still shuffling. "We'll play every night, and I'll coach you every night here in the room."

"Coach me?" Sounds like . . . work. Besides, I thought I was a natural. "I thought you said I was a natural."

"You're good," he says. "You're great at running some of the numbers in your head. But intuition is important, too, and you also need to understand the importance of pot odds." He sits up straight. "You need to start calculating *all* the odds in your head, not just of winning, but of how much you'd be risking to make what, so that you can combine that with your intuition and the card combinations."

He gets up and flops onto the bed, where he shuffles the cards and then deals two hands onto the fluffy white comforter. He looks at me, clearly indicating that I should sit next to him. I hesitate. I shouldn't even be *in* this hotel room, much less sitting on the bed with him.

But I sit anyway, and we spend the next hour and a half going over percentages and odds. He's right that there's a lot more to it than I originally thought. Not only do I have to take into consideration what I have in my hand and balance that with what's on the board and what other people might have, I also have to pay attention to how much is in the pot. If I'm almost sure someone has beat me but I've already invested a lot of chips, sometimes it's worth it to throw in a little more on the chance that I might win a big pot. It's all about risk versus reward.

The good news is I'm lighting quick at doing the math in my head, so it doesn't take me long to look at a hand, look at the board, look at the pot, and calculate the odds. The hard part is trying to guess what the other people's odds are based on what *they're* doing. Especially since you have to make pretty quick decisions, and there can be eight other people at the table.

I'm so caught up in what Cole's teaching me that when I finally look up, it's already almost midnight.

"Holy shit," I say, looking at the clock on the table near the bed. "It's already twelve."

"Past your curfew?" Cole asks, smiling. I'm about to say, "Um, yeah," but then realize that's probably not the best way to shake my reputation of being naïve and childish. I start to freak out a little, but then figure if my parents were really looking for me, they would have tried my phone. Besides, they definitely should both be in bed by now, and ever since that night when my car broke down, my mom hasn't been checking in on me. Just as I thought, my phone has only one text, from Mackenzie. It says, "Have fun! Don't do anything I wouldn't do, can't wait to hear all about it." That's followed by a smiley and about six million *x*'s and *o*'s.

"You ready to go down to the poker room?" Cole asks. He's gathering up the cards, and one of them falls out of the stack onto the bed, and as he reaches for it, his hand brushes against my arm. He's really close now, and when he pulls back, he keeps his face near mine.

"Yes," I say, trying to sound calm. He's so close that I can feel his breath on my face, and his lips are like two inches away from mine. I start to get nervous, figuring that if I can see *his* lips so well, then he can see *mine,* and I wonder if he can tell that my lips are chapped, because my lips tend to get chapped really easily, and usually I keep Chap Stick on them, but I couldn't this time because I put on all that lipstick, and I'm wondering why I even care, because I don't even like Cole, and then all of a sudden he's moving closer and his lips are on mine.

And then his mouth opens slightly and his tongue is in my mouth and we fall down to the bed and we're kissing and his hands are on my back and I can feel my body responding to his.

I pull away from the kiss first, not because I want

to, but because it seems like the right thing to do. I mean, that's crazy, me kissing Cole. It doesn't make sense. I like Max. Actually, no. I don't like Max. I don't like *anyone*. I like being alone, thank you very much. Single and drama free. Besides, isn't Cole kind of like my boss now? I don't think it's the best idea to be hooking up with your boss. Nothing good can come of that.

"We should go," I say, sitting up. I smooth my hair and look at the ground. "Downstairs. So I can put what you taught me into action."

"Right," he says, grinning at me. "I bet you just can't wait to put what I've taught you into action."

"Stop being such an ass," I say. I stand up and Cole follows me out the door and onto the elevator.

"I'm going to sit with you," he says as the doors shut. I watch the numbers start their descent, and I get more excited as we get closer to the poker room. "At the same table, I mean."

"Okay," I say, suddenly nervous. I don't want him sitting with me. It feels like too much scrutiny. The other night, when I wanted him to sit with me, he didn't want to. Now, all of a sudden, he wants to bring me out there. "But why?"

"So you can watch me," he says. "And I can watch you."

Great. My heart starts beating at about three hundred miles a minute.

We get right into a three-six table. And for once, I have to agree that Cole might be right. About my outfit. The guys at the table react to me in a different way than the guys did the other night. They don't take me seriously, yet at the same time, they act flustered around me, like everything's different now that a girl in a sexy outfit is sitting at their table.

Cole sits down a few minutes after I do, and we pretend like we don't know each other.

He raises his eyebrows, and gives me little looks and signals that make me slow down, think, and run all the numbers in my head.

And when the guy next to me orders a glass of red wine, I follow suit and do the same. So that's how I spend the night, drinking a little wine, playing poker, watching Cole, and feeling sophisticated and exhilarated. Every time another pile of chips gets pushed across the table to me, my heart beats fast, and every time I have to fold a hand, my heart sinks and I wait impatiently until I can get into another one.

It's a complete and total rush, and I love the feeling of the cards beneath my fingers, the excitement in the air, and the knowing that anything could happen. By the end of the night, I've won three hundred dollars.

And by the time I leave the casino, it's five-thirty in the morning.

9

*O*nce I'm on my way home, the three hundred dollars tucked neatly into my purse, my high starts to fade. Fast. One, not only have I *made out with Cole,* but two, I have been out *all night.* Playing poker. Which means that I will now have to figure out a way to sneak inside my house, get ready for school, and head off without anyone's being the wiser. Of course, I'll be going to school on pretty much no sleep, but if I can just get through the morning, I think I might be able to skip my afternoon classes by faking sick, then come home and take a nap before work.

I'm pretty confident in my sneak-in-and-sneak-out-to-school plan, until I open the door to my house and find Robyn sitting at the table, a book open in front of her.

"Oh, hello," she says, looking up at me.

"Oh, hello," I say. I feel my mouth go dry, and my face gets hot. Lying to Leonardo is one thing, but fooling my sister . . . I've never really done it before this whole casino thing. And I'm not sure if I can pull it off. "I was just, um, out taking a walk before school." I give her a big smile, like "Isn't fitness great?"

She raises her eyebrows. "Dressed like that?" I look down at the dress I'm wearing, the one I stole from her closet. It's now totally disheveled from all the, um, hanging out I was doing on Cole's bed, and it smells of the general disgustingness that is the air of the casino.

"Fine," I say, deciding to give her limited information. "I was out, but if you tell Mom or Dad, I'm going to kill you."

"Out doing what?" she asks, excited. She slams her book shut and looks like she's ready to settle in for a sister-to-sister chat.

"Just, you know," I say, "out." I figure this should suffice, since I've never asked Robyn where she's gone when she's out late and needs me to cover for her. Which, by the way, I've done tons of times. Of course, it's pretty much known that she's always out with

Leonardo, so it's not like what she's done or where she's been is some big secret. I, on the other hand, have never snuck in late at night after being out with a guy, so this is kind of a big deal.

"With a guy?" Robyn asks. Her voice is all singsongy.

"Yes," I say. Not a lie.

"With Max?" She grins, and I feel bad, because I don't want to lie to her, but I can't tell her the truth now, can I? So I just smile in what I hope is a mysterious way that she takes to mean "yes" but is technically not an answer, and then say, "What are you doing up so early, anyway?"

"I have class at eight," she says. "And we're having a test, so I decided to do a little early-morning studying." She glances at the clock and frowns. "Actually, Leonardo was supposed to be here by now to take me to the library."

"I'm sure he'll be here soon," I say. I grab a protein shake out of the fridge (they're my dad's, but I figure I'm going to need some kind of energy boost if I'm going to make it through the morning) and head upstairs, where I wash my face, brush my teeth, and pull a brush through my hair. I change into jeans and a sweater, then head back out the door to school.

I don't even see my mom or my dad, and I get to school half an hour early. *And* I don't even feel tired. Is it possible that this might really be that easy? That I'm going to be able to get away with playing poker every night, that I'll be able to make hundreds of dollars and stop when I have enough for Wellesley, and that I won't get into trouble? I mean, it seems completely unlikely and unfair, but so far so good.

I'm so busy pondering the possibilities of this throughout first period that I don't realize that Parvati has followed me out of math. I'm at my locker, getting my books for my next class (and trying to resist the urge to check my phone to see if Cole has texted me), when she finally comes up to me.

"Helllooo, Shannon," she says, leaning against the locker next to mine. I jump.

"Oh," I say. "Hi." I'm really not in the mood to hear about her and Max, or her and Wellesley, or her and the math scholarship, or her and [insert anything here]. So I do my best to try and ignore her, even though I know it's futile. Parvati does not take hints. But then she reaches over and slams my locker door shut before I'm even done getting my books.

"Hey," I say. "I wasn't done in there!"

"What," she demands, crossing her arms over her chest, "happened between you and Max?"

Oh. My. God. Okay. Deep breath. There is no need to panic. I mean, there's no way she could know about me and Max, right? God, what if she knows about me and Max? What if Max told her? Why would Max tell her? What guy is that stupid? Unless he's one of those guys with tons of integrity, ugh. Wait a minute. If Max told Parvati what happened, why would she be asking *me* what happened? She would already know.

More likely, she *heard* about something happening and is now trying to figure it out.

"Um," I say, stalling for time and information. "What do you mean?"

"I *mean,*" she says, "that you were seen having a fight with him in the hall yesterday." She jams her finger into my chest, and I take a step back. We were seen? By *who*? It was early in the morning; the halls were completely deserted. Although I guess maybe we *were* being pretty loud, and now that I think about it, I do remember seeing a few kids wandering around. But I thought they were just some freshman walkers.

"Oh, *that,*" I say. "That was nothing." I give a little chuckle and wave my hand at her dismissively. "We weren't even fighting, really. All we did was have a little bit of a yell. Not even a yell. It was more like some raised voices." Parvati doesn't look convinced. "It was nothing," I repeat lamely.

"What was nothing?" Parvati demands, and suddenly she looks kind of . . . wild. Her hair is all sticking up (Parvati's hair is usually very smooth), and her eyes have this crazed look in them. I've never seen her like this, and I start to become a little frightened, even though she's only five foot one.

"The thing that happened in the hall," I whisper.

"What *DID* HAPPEN IN THE HALL?" Parvati's having a bit of a yell herself at this point, and now she's pretty close to my face. I have a bad feeling that if I don't give her the right answer, she might just go crazy. Maybe even punch me.

157

"Now," she says. "You better tell me, and tell me good." Tell her good? Wow. That's a little . . . extreme.

"Look," I say. "We were, uh, having a fight about tutoring. Max thought I wasn't giving it my all, and so he got a little heated with me." I sigh and push my hair out of my face. I roll my eyes as if to say, "You know how Max is about his math."

She narrows her eyes at me. "I don't believe you," she finally says.

"Um, you don't?"

"No," she says. She studies me up and down and then crosses her arms over her green polo shirt. "Because if you two were just fighting about the tutoring, then why did he break up with me?"

"Why did he *what*?" I ask. Parvati and Max broke up? My heart beats a little faster as I wonder if maybe it had anything to do with me.

"WHY DID HE BREAK UP WITH ME?" Parvati yells. Several people turn to stare.

"Walk," I say, grabbing her shirt and pulling her down the hall with me. I lead her into the alcove by the stairs. "Listen," I say, "I don't know why he broke up with you." And then, all at once, the fight seems to drain right out of her. Her whole face crumples up like tissue paper, and the next thing I know, she's crying.

"I don't know, either," she says. "I just . . . I just wish . . ."

Wow. This is really awkward, having an emotional moment with your math archenemy, the ex-girlfriend of the guy you used to be in love with, in the alcove where people usually go to make out.

"I just wish . . ." Parvati takes a big sniff.

"You just wish what?" I say. I move in so I can hear her, but Parvati seems to think this means I want to hug her, and she steps in close to me. I place my arms awkwardly around her back. Oh, God.

"I just wish it hadn't happened," she says. "I mean, we were so happy together. We even had a great weekend."

"What did he say *exactly*?" I ask, wondering if it makes me a horrible person that I'm really hoping their breakup had something to do with me.

"He didn't give me a good reason," she says, sniffing again. "He just kept saying he needed space."

"It's okay," I tell her. I try to smooth her hair down in the back.

"It is?" she asks.

"It is," I say. "It'll all work out one way or the other."

"It will?" she asks.

"Yes," I say. She pulls away from me, and I reach into my bag and hand her a tissue. She blows her nose obediently. "Here, take this." I pull out my iPod and shove it into her hands. "Listen to the playlist that's called Boys Suck."

She looks at me blankly. "Boys Suck?" she repeats.

"Yeah," I say. "I know it's not all that original, but I think you'll like it."

"Thanks," she says, slipping the buds into her ears and scrolling through the songs.

"And, Parvati," I say, "if you want to know why Max broke up with you, then you should ask him again. You deserve an explanation."

♥ ♠ ♣ ♦

I know Max has second period free, and that he usually spends it in the library. I know this because once (okay, twice), I accidentally maybe on purpose followed him. But that was at the beginning of the year, when I was still holding out hope that we might be friends again.

But whatever. If I just *happen* to be in the library second period, and if I just *happen* to see Max waiting in line to check out a book, and if I just *happen* to go talk to him, it's totally fine, since:

a) I don't even like him anymore. I mean, I just kissed someone else last night. Still. I smooth my hair self-consciously and hope he doesn't notice the dark circles under my eyes.

b) I need to tell him to talk to Parvati and tell her there's nothing going on with us, before I end up in the middle of all their drama.

"We need to talk," I say, walking up to him in the library checkout line.

"Oh, *now* you want to talk," he says, repeating my words from yesterday. At the front of the line, a harried-looking student worker is trying to check people out. Why is the line so long, anyway? Who still checks books out of the school library?

"Look," I say, "you need to talk to Parvati, you need to give her a reason why you broke up with her, because she thinks it has something to do with me."

There's a few seconds of silence, and for a moment, I'm almost thinking (hoping) that he's going to say it *does* have something to do with me, but then he says, "Why did you lie to me about your fake ID?" I'm thrown by the change in topic.

"What are you talking about?" I ask, frowning.

"You told me you were using the fake ID so that you could get a job at the casino to pay for Wellesley."

"I was," I say. "I mean, I did." Geez. What is the deal with all the questions? I'm the one who's come here to confront *him*, to tell him he'd better start being honest with his girlfriend. I don't owe him anything. He's not even my friend! He's just a guy who I *used* to be friends with, who I accidentally kissed, and who I maybe kind of sort of still like. No! I mean, who I kind of sort of *don't* still like. No, who I *definitely* don't still like, because–

"Then how come Chris Harmon saw you at the casino last night, playing poker with a bunch of guys?"

"That," I say haughtily, "is none of your business." Also, how is everyone at the casino all the time? First Leonardo, now Chris Harmon. Really, the place has to get a better system of IDing people. I don't know why I was so nervous about my fake birth certificate; they're obviously just letting anyone in. If I wasn't getting in with a fake ID, I would totally call the news and tip them off.

"Are you . . . Shannon, do you have a gambling problem?" He's looking at me seriously, and I gape at him. Is he kidding me?

"Are you *kidding* me?" I ask.

A sophomore girl in front of us in line turns around and shushes us.

"Sorry," I say. I turn back to Max. "Are you kidding me?" I whisper.

"No, I just . . ."

"I do not have a gambling problem," I say. "And not that it's any of your business, but if you must know, yes, I was at the casino playing poker. Who cares? Lots of people play poker."

"Fine," Max says. "It's not a big deal, I was just worried about you, that's all." He's at the front of the line now, and he sets his book down in front of the student worker, who opens the book and scans it. My heart catches in my chest. Max was worried about me? But then I remember that Max has my number, and if he was so worried about me, he could have called.

"You were worried about me?" I ask. "Just all of a sudden?"

"No," he says. "Not all of a sudden. You're my friend."

I look at him incredulously. "We're *friends*?" I ask. "Because that's news to me. Friends call each other. Friends talk to each other and hang out. And friends don't kiss each other and then never talk again!"

"Max Heller?" the student worker says, looking

between the two of us nervously. "Um, you have an overdue library book."

"Oh, Jesus," Max says. "What book is it?"

"The Stand," the worker says. "Stephen King?"

"Yeah, I know who wrote it," Max says, sounding annoyed. He pulls out his wallet. "Can I just pay for it?"

"And besides," I say, getting angrier, "you don't have to worry about me. Because I was there with a guy."

"A guy?" Max frowns.

"Yeah," I say. "My new boyfriend." Granted, that's a little bit of a stretch. Even I know that one kiss does not a boyfriend make. But I'm not going to say that to Max. "I was there with my new hookup" definitely doesn't pack the same punch.

"Your new *boyfriend*?" Max looks at me incredulously. "You have a new boyfriend after you kissed me the other night?"

"I. Was. *Drunk,*" I hiss. "And you kissed me, too."

"You were drunk?" he asks, ignoring the part about his kissing me, too. "And so your lips just happened to fall onto mine?" His voice is a little raised now, and the student worker, whose name tag reads "Ron," starts to look super-nervous.

"Yes, you can pay for it," Ron says. "Twenty-seven ninety-five."

"They didn't *fall* onto yours," I say. "I was tipsy. I can't be held responsible for what I did the other night.

163

It was nothing, it was just"—I wave my hand—"a drunken mistake." The words almost catch in my throat, but I'm able to push them through.

"Fine," Max says. I'm not sure if he's talking to me or Ron.

"Fine?"

"Fine that you have a boyfriend now, and fine, I'll pay twenty-seven ninety-five for the stupid book." He pulls two twenties out of his wallet and drops them onto the counter.

"I'll have to get you some change," Ron says. The idea seems to send him into a little bit of a panic.

"And," I say to Max, "you don't have to worry about it, because these things happen. Kind of like last summer, when you kissed me and then had a girlfriend a couple of weeks later."

He looks at me for a long second, and for a moment, I think he's going to say something else. He *wants* to say something else, I think, but then the look leaves his face, and he turns around and walks away, leaving his money and his book on the counter.

And I turn and walk toward the door on the other side of the library, blinking back tears.

10

"*T*his is so good," Mackenzie says. We're on our break at work later that night, eating sandwiches in the café. A BLT and fries for her, a chicken sandwich from home for me, although I'm not really that hungry and have spent most of the time sipping my soda and pushing my chips around my plate. "In fact, this might be the best sandwich *ever*."

"Mmhmm," I say, trying to resist the urge to lay my head down on the table and close my eyes. I skipped my afternoon classes and snuck home to take a nap, but apparently the four hours I spent sleeping didn't really help, since I've felt like keeling over for most of the night. Plus I cannot stop thinking about Max and our altercation in the library and his breakup with Parvati and what the whole thing means.

Which is so totally stupid. I have Cole now. Cole, who is very sexy in that bad-boy kind of way. Cole, who had me in his bed last night, kissed me, and didn't even try anything. Wait. Why *didn't* he try anything?

"Hey, Mackenzie," I say. "If you were making out with a guy, and he didn't try anything, would you be upset?"

"What do you mean?" She frowns and takes a sip of her iced tea. Her shell-pink lipstick stays perfectly applied.

"I mean, say you were on a guy's bed, and you kissed, but then you pulled away, and he didn't even try to stop you."

Mackenzie looks shocked. "That wouldn't happen," she says, shaking her blond head vehemently. "Guys don't do that." She takes a big bite of her sandwich and chews noisily.

"But what if one of them did?" I persist.

"I would think he was gay," she says, and then shrugs. Hmmm. "Are you going to eat that?" She points to the rest of the chicken on wheat bread sitting on my tray.

"No," I say, pushing it toward her. "Take it." I'm too

anxious to eat. I haven't heard from Cole all day, so I have no idea if we're meeting up tonight or what. And there's no way I'm going to call him, because, you know, we made out last night. I sigh and pull my phone out again and check it. Mackenzie takes my sandwich, pulls off the top piece of bread, and gets to work squeezing about five million packets of mayonnaise onto it.

"Why are you phone obsessing?" she asks.

"I'm not," I say.

"Ooh, I get it," she says. "You made out with whoever you were going to meet last night, and now you're hoping he's going to text you."

"Sort of," I say.

"Who's the guy?"

"Just this guy," I say.

"Well, I wouldn't worry if you don't hear from him tonight," she says. "Haven't you ever heard of the three-day rule?"

"No," I say.

"It's basically this rule where if you give a guy your number, or hang out with a guy, then he's supposed to wait three days to call you, so that he doesn't seem desperate."

"That's lame," I say. I don't tell her that Cole had better not take three days, since I'm a part of his underground poker society and that would really mess with my plan of winning a lot of money tonight. Not to mention that I just don't want to be blown off after making out with him.

"It *is* totally lame," Mackenzie agrees. "Which is why it's so great that Filipe called me this morning, even though we just hung out last night." She takes a bite of my sandwich, and some mayonnaise squirts out the other end of the bread. "We're totally on the right track."

Mackenzie had a great time on her date with Filipe last night. I know because she's been talking about it nonstop since she got to work. He took her to dinner (and paid, which I guess was a big deal, since Lance never paid) and then to a movie ("Lance always hated movies, and wouldn't even go with me, and that is definitely not compromising") and then to the bookstore ("Filipe loves to read, so we got cappuccinos and he looked at books and I read *Us Weekly*. It was so fun to just be able to hang out and not be out at a club or something, you know?"). He took her home and kissed her good night and called her this morning, and according to her, she's in love.

"That is very gentlemanly," I say. I actually don't mind that Mackenzie is talking so much about her date. It makes me happy to see her happy, even though she's kind of, halfway, a little bit backhandedly dissing Cole for not calling me today. But whatevs. I wouldn't be surprised if I never heard from him again—he's pretty good at disappearing.

But at the end of my shift, Cole is waiting for me. And he pulls me to the side of the casino, where no one from work is watching, and kisses me. His lips taste like cherries and alcohol, and the kiss is amazing.

"Hey," I breathe.

"Hey," he says, pulling away and looking at me. "So are you ready to play?"

♥　♠　♣　♦

I change into a pair of really tight jeans and a red shirt that has a plunging back and a plunging neckline. I do my best to replicate the makeup and hair Mackenzie gave me, and then slip my feet into high open-toed silver shoes. My outfit is courtesy of Robyn's closet.

Everything goes down the same as it did last night. I sit at a table with Cole, and once again, we pretend not to know each other while he helps me by giving me little signals. I get slightly nervous when it seems like one of the other guys at the table sees us eyeing each other, so I strike up a fake conversation with Cole, and I flirt with the suspicious guy for good measure.

Pretty soon, we're all laughing and acting like friends.

Later in the night, I get a weird feeling that maybe it's cheating a little bit to have Cole keep giving me suggestive looks. I mean, why should I be helped when no one else is being helped? Also, at one point I feel like maybe he folds his hand just so I can win, but I tell myself that's crazy.

Cole's just helping me learn to read people and teaching me more about the important statistics and calculating the pot odds. And it's not like we have an *official* system worked out or anything. There are just times when I can tell he wants me to think about a call before I make it. And he's not going to be doing it forever—just until I'm ready to be on my own.

Around two in the morning, I decide to cash out, and I head to the side of the casino to turn in my chips. I've won another two hundred dollars tonight.

"Hey," Cole says, running up to me while I'm waiting for the elevator. "Good night tonight."

"Thanks," I say. "Good night to you, too." I step into the elevator and push the button for the parking garage, but Cole follows me in and pushes the button for the hotel.

"No, not good night," he says. "I mean you had a good night. At the tables."

"So did you," I say. Cole won about five hundred dollars. He shrugs, like it's no big deal.

"Where are you going?" he asks, his dark eyes looking me up and down. I'm reminded of the night we met and how weird it was to be in the elevator with him. I'm not sure if it's the outfit or that I just felt so in control at the tables, but I don't feel strange now at all.

"Home," I say. "It's late."

But when the elevator gets to the parking garage, Cole pushes the door close button before I can get out. As the doors close again and the elevator starts making its way up to his room, I lean against the back wall until he comes over to me.

"Hi," he says. And then his lips are on mine.

♥ ♠ ♣ ♦

That's how it goes. For the next three weeks, my life is school, casino, poker, school, casino, poker. I have a couple of rough nights, when I don't do very well, and a couple of great nights, when I do really, really well. At the end of each night, Cole gives me my stake of the money, in cash. And in three weeks, I've made eight thousand dollars. Eight. Thousand. Dollars. At this rate, I'll have all the money I need in just a few months, and I can quit poker forever.

"What are you doing with your money, Shannon Card?" Cole asks me one night as we're lying in his hotel bed after a particularly great night at the tables.

"Saving it," I murmur into his hair.

"*All* of it?" He sounds shocked. He twirls a strand of my hair around his finger. Cole and I spend a lot of time here, in the hotel room, watching TV, ordering room service, and making out. I usually end up dozing a little bit and then sneaking home for a few hours of sleep before I have to be at school. On the weekends, I don't see Cole or go to the casino, so I catch up on my sleep then. And my homework. That's the only downside to this. My grades have been slipping, and I need to do a better job of focusing on my work. Otherwise it won't matter that I'm making tons of money, because I won't be allowed into Wellesley.

It's just so hard to stay focused. It seems like every night I make a vow to myself that I'm only going to play for an hour, and I end up at the tables all night. I'm getting better, out on my own now, without Cole sitting next to me, and I don't want to lose that momentum.

"I need it," I say now. "For school." Cole kisses me on the forehead and doesn't push. Actually, besides when it comes to poker stuff, Cole doesn't push at all. About anything. He's never asked me about my family, or about my friends, or about whether I like my job at the casino. We play poker, we talk about poker, we order room service, and we make out.

"Hey," I say, leaning up on one elbow. "How come I haven't met any of the other members of Aces Up?"

"You will," he says. He reaches behind him, grabs the remote off the end table, and points it at the TV. GSN comes on the screen. They're showing a rerun of *High-Stakes Poker*.

"Let's watch *Real World*," I suggest. "They're doing a marathon."

He looks at me like I'm crazy. "But this is the newest episode," he says.

"Yeah, but we've already watched it five times."

Cole pulls me closer. "You have to study, Shannon Card," he tells me.

This makes me cranky for some reason. All we ever do is watch poker. Actually, all we ever do is lie in this bed. We don't go out to dinner or to movies or anything. Mackenzie's new boyfriend, Filipe, has been whisking her all around town, taking her to dinner, to plays, to meet his parents. He even bought her this really cute beaded necklace at a street fair they went to. A street fair! How cute and fun does that sound? I haven't even been to Cole's dorm room. He prefers staying in the casino hotel, and pays for the room by the month.

We've pushed past "just kissing" into third-base territory. You'd think that would at least warrant hanging out on the weekends. I sigh and close my eyes, and pretty soon, the TV lulls me to sleep.

♥ ♠ ♣ ♦

I'm woken up by my cell phone ringing, and I force my eyes to focus on the clock next to the bed. Seven a.m. Damn. I'm supposed to be out of here by now, on my way home so I can sleep for a little bit before school. I always set the alarm for four, but it must not have gone off for some reason. I'm going to be late for school, not to mention that my parents or Robyn might be wondering where I am.

My phone stops ringing and then starts again. Robyn.

"Hello?" I say. I grab my jeans off the floor and force my legs into them, almost falling over in the process.

"Where the hell are you?" she demands.

"Um, sorry," I say, trying to whisper so that I don't wake up Cole. "I went back to my friend Mackenzie's house after work, and I fell asleep there." The lie sounds hollow, even to me, and on the bed, Cole turns over in his sleep.

"Yeah, well, Mom and Dad are freaking out," she

says. She lowers her voice, I assume so that they can't hear. "They know you never came home last night. Mom didn't even go to work, she's so worried."

My heart feels like it's stopped beating. And then, a second later, it starts beating super-fast. "How mad are they?" I ask. "Like, on a scale of one to ten, one being they're a little annoyed and ten being I might be living on the street soon." I look around the room for the shirt I wore last night, but it's nowhere to be found.

"They're worried," she says. "And I am, too. Shannon, Leonardo saw you at the casino last night. He said you were playing poker until really late, and then you left with some guy."

My breath catches in my chest, and I try to swallow. "That's crazy," I say, forcing a laugh. "I was at work at the Rusty Nail, and then I went over to my friend Mackenzie's house, I told you." I feel bad for lying to my sister, but it surprises me that I don't feel as bad as I probably should. I pick up one of Cole's hoodies off the floor, pull it over my head, and shove my arms through the sleeves.

"So you weren't at the casino?" she asks. "With a guy? Wearing a super-short black skirt?"

"No!" I say. Cole stirs again in bed and then sits up and looks at me.

"What time is it?" he mumbles, blinking sleepily.

"Look," I say quickly to Robyn, "I have to go, I'm going to be late for school."

"All right," Robyn says, sighing. "But, Shannon, you should call Mom."

♥ ♠ ♣ ♦

Twenty minutes later, I'm pulling into the parking lot of school, having talked my mom down from a ledge ("We were about to call the *police,* Shannon, you have no idea how worried we were!") and somehow convinced her not to be mad. Well, she's a little bit mad. Just not crazy mad. I think I'll be able to talk to her later and make everything okay. But still. That was a close one. And honestly pretty stupid on my part. I mean, up until this point, it has pretty much been a miracle that I haven't been caught. It was only a matter of time until something like this was going to happen, and I *cannot* let it happen again.

As if all this stress isn't enough, when I get to school, Parvati is at my locker with my iPod. We haven't really talked since that day in the stairwell, and to tell you the truth, I've been so busy that I kind of forgot she still had it.

"Hey," she says. "I wanted to give this back to you. Sorry I held on to it for so long."

"No problem," I say. I wind up the headphones and slide it into my bag. "Did it help at all?"

"Yeah," she says.

We stand there awkwardly for a moment. "So, uh, how are you doing?" I ask. She looks much better than she did a few weeks ago. Her hair is pulled back into a smooth ponytail, and she's wearing a brown blazer, crisp jeans, and matching brown flats. Her nails are painted a really dark pink, and she's lost the crazy look in her eyes.

"I'm good," she says. "A lot better. I talked to Max, and he told me what happened."

"He did?" Uh-oh. So that's why she decided to wait for me this morning. I'm thankful I have my iPod back, since I could totally see her wanting to strangle me with the cord. I swallow and wait for her to go crazy. I mean, I tried to *kiss* her *boyfriend*. This is definitely an act. Parvati's pretending she has it all together, and just waiting to smack me or pull my hair or start screaming at me and creating a scene.

"Yeah," she says. She readjusts her bag on her shoulder. "So I wanted to say thanks."

"Thanks?" I ask warily, waiting for her to finish it up with "for being a skank whore" or "for making it okay to do *this*" followed by a good kick in the shins.

"Yeah," she says, looking at the ground. "You know, for not kissing him back."

What? What is she talking about? Of course I kissed him back! I mean, no, I didn't kiss him back, I *initiated* the kissing. And if he *had* initiated it, *of course* I would have kissed him back. Plus initiating the kiss is way worse than not kissing him back. *Or* kissing him back. I'm confused.

I don't know what to say, so I settle on "Oh?"

"He told me he tried to kiss you, and you didn't kiss him back, and I really appreciate that."

"Well, you're welcome," I say. I feel horrible. I'm a horrible, horrible liar. Parvati is being nothing but nice to me, and I'm just lying. Over and over. Right to her face. Of course, I'm not technically lying, since Max is

176

the one who started the lie. But I'm going along with it. It's like lying by omission. Which is just as bad. I saw it on *Tyra*.

"I'm soo excited for quarter grades to come out," Parvati says, her face suddenly brightening. "I know I killed it in math." She checks her watch. "Well, I'm late to meet Josh. He's going to help me with my math. He got a five on his AP exam, and he's my private tutor. He's going to Yale next year, so that will be hard if I get into Wellesley." She sighs and fiddles with the strap of her bag. "I'll probably have to get a new car, one that gets good gas mileage." And then she takes off down the hall without even saying goodbye or asking about my math grade. Probably because she knows how horribly I'm doing (three failed quizzes and a not-so-stellar unit test grade) and loves it that she can imply I'm not even a threat.

Okay, so maybe I don't feel that bad about the lying.

♥ ♠ ♣ ♦

Must. Not. Text. Max. In math, I stare at the back of his neck from my seat one row over and three back. And I totally want to text him. Just so I can say, you know, thanks for not throwing me under the bus. One little text. That wouldn't hurt anything, would it? Just one little tiny text. It would be polite, even. The right thing to do. And I haven't really been doing many of the right things lately, so this could be a good start. Turning over a new leaf, if you will.

Besides, we haven't talked since that day in the

library, and it might be nice to just smooth things over. Not forgive him or anything—that would be ridiculous—but just make it clear that we shouldn't hate each other.

I reach into my bag and pull my phone out, hiding it under my desk while I tap out the message. "Thx for not telling Parvati what really happened," I say. "U saved me from a J. Crew ass whoopin." I press send and hope he thinks it's funny.

A second later, I see him check his phone through the pocket of his hoodie. He frowns, and then his fingers go flying over the keyboard.

"No problem," his text says. I'm about to text him back, but then I watch as he shuts his phone off and puts it in his bag. Okay, then.

♥ ♠ ♣ ♦

On my way out of math, Ms. Kellogg pulls me aside and asks if she can talk to me. It's never a good thing when your teacher asks you to stay after class. Unfortunately, I don't even have the luxury of being able to drive myself crazy figuring out what she could possibly want to talk to me about. I already know. I've failed my last three quizzes, and my last test grade was a sixty-seven.

"Sit down, Shannon," she says. Uh-oh. I've never been asked to sit down before in Ms. Kellogg's class. Usually when I come to talk to her, we have nice little chats, where we're more like friends than teacher and student. Once, at the beginning of the year, I even let her borrow my *Us Weekly*. (It was the one with the Eva

Longoria and Tony Parker cheating rumors.) But she doesn't look too friendly or like she's thinking about celeb gossip right now.

"What's going on?" I ask, plastering a smile on my face. My just-thought-up and newly decided-on plan is to pretend like a few bad grades are not a big deal. Which they aren't, really, when you think about it. A lot of people get bad grades. Bill Gates didn't even go to college. Of course, there is the whole "if I don't keep my grades up, my admission to Wellesley will be revoked" thing, but they haven't fallen *that* bad. I mean, it's just a few quizzes. And a test. And she said I could do extra credit.

"I think you know that your grades haven't been what I've come to expect from you." She leans across her desk, and her blouse dips down, giving me a glimpse of the black lacy bra she's wearing underneath. No wonder boys can't concentrate in this class.

"I know," I say, nodding seriously. "And I'm sorry. It's *totally* unlike me. But it's only been a couple of quizzes, and I'm confident I can turn it around." I give her a smile. If there's one thing that poker has taught me, it's that it's all about the body language.

"It was three quizzes," she says. "And a unit test." Way to have a perfect memory. Geez.

"Well, I'm going to do better," I say, infusing my voice with confidence.

"Shannon, why didn't you tell me that you stopped working with Max?" she says, apparently deciding to throw me a curveball. She leans back in her chair, crosses her arms, and waits.

"Um, we're not exactly . . . I mean . . ." Something tells me "we almost kissed and then it was awkward" isn't going to fly here. Finally, I settle for "Um, I didn't know I had to tell you."

"Well, you're getting extra credit for tutoring, so if you stopped doing it, you probably should have told me. Otherwise you're getting extra credit for nothing, which is a lot like cheating." Her eyes are serious. I've never seen Ms. Kellogg like this. Suddenly, she's this hard-ass teacher instead of my friend. It's . . . a little scary.

"I didn't mean to cheat," I say, horrified that she would think that. "I just didn't know that I needed to, um, alert you right away. Or I definitely would have." And it's true. I would have told her immediately if I'd known it was that big of a deal.

"Okay." She looks disappointed, and I swallow hard. Suddenly, I feel like I want to get out of here, like I'm all claustrophobic and can't stand to be in this class-room for one more second.

"Is that all?" I ask, standing up.

"Yes," she says. But she's looking at me seriously, and then her face softens. "Shannon, if you ever need someone to talk to . . ."

"I'm fine," I say. "I told you, I've just been sick and I had a couple of bad tests. I'm going to turn it around, I promise." And then I head out of the room before I start to cry.

♥ ♠ ♣ ♦

That night after work, Cole takes me out to dinner at this super-expensive seafood place in the casino. This is completely unexpected, since Cole and I don't do dinner, really. ("He doesn't take you anywhere?" Mackenzie screeched at me earlier today. I couldn't let her know that he's doing quite enough by teaching me how to make tens of thousands of dollars, and that by the time we're finished playing poker, we're too tired to do anything except go lie in bed. Also, there was no reasoning with her, because ever since she started dating Filipe, she's like a walking poster for what you should want in a relationship. Honestly, her self-esteem has gone to ridiculously high levels. It's kind of scary.)

"Can I order whatever I want?" I ask Cole, my eyes scanning the menu. Then I remember that Cole drives an Escalade and probably isn't going to be too hurt if I order lobster. Not that I would. Order lobster, I mean. But that's only because I don't really like lobster. Too much work and mess.

"Of course you can," Cole says, reaching over and taking my hand. I smile. See? Who needs dumb Max Heller? Cole is perfectly fine. Cole is a gentleman. Cole is taking me out to dinner and letting me order whatever I want. Cole is a man. Max Heller is a boy who works at a gas station. Not that there's anything wrong with working at a gas station. To tell the truth, I find it a little bit . . . sexy. Max, out there working with his hands, making sure that everyone's cars are functioning properly. Max in a wife beater, all sweaty, rolling himself out from under some car and standing up, holding lots of . . . tools.

I shake my head and push the image out of my mind. I tell myself the only reason I'm even *thinking* about Max is because Parvati brought him up today. For the past few weeks, I've been fine, living a Max-free existence and being perfectly happy about it.

I order the grilled haddock, even though I really want the fish-and-chips, because this strikes me as the kind of place where that sort of thing is frowned upon. Like you're at a nice seafood restaurant, so you shouldn't ruin it by ordering fried fish, which you can get anywhere. I think it's comparable to putting ketchup on steak. It's okay, though. I mean, I should probably get used to it, since once I become flush with cash, I'm going to have to start eating with a little more class.

Cole orders the lobster bake.

"So how was school today?" I ask him once the waiter has cleared the area. I figure we're out on our first "real" date, so we should talk about what people talk about when they're on dates. And that definitely does not include what we usually talk about, which is poker. And money. And money. And poker.

"Fine," he says.

"Just fine?" I say. "Nothing interesting or exciting? What were your lectures about?"

"Who cares?" Cole asks, leaning back in his chair

and grinning at me. "I'm not going to be using my degree, anyway."

"You mean because ninety percent of college graduates end up in a field that's completely unrelated to their major?" Not sure where I heard that statistic. I think maybe I read it somewhere. No, it was one of those things that some college recruiter told me in an effort to get me to apply to his second-tier school that had a horrible English department. I outsmarted him by telling him I'd rather have a degree I wasn't using from Wellesley than a degree I wasn't using from his dumb-ass school. I didn't say it quite like that, but close enough.

"No, Shannon Card," Cole says. He takes a sip of the red wine the waiter has just placed on our table. "Because I'm going to be playing poker."

I frown. "Even after you're done with school?" I never really considered this as a possibility. I figured that once Cole had his degree, he'd be done with the whole poker thing. I mean, who wants to be a poker player? That's not, like, a goal. Is it?

"Yeah," he says. "Same as I'm doing now." He takes another sip of wine and then pours more into his glass.

"Oh," I say. "I just figured . . ."

"I'm making way more doing this than I would at any dumb office job." He looks at me and smiles. "Not to mention it's way more fun."

"That's cool," I say. But there's a weird feeling in my stomach. I assumed that Cole looked at Aces Up the same way I did—as something he was doing until he made enough money that he didn't have to anymore. But now that I know this is his chosen career path, the whole thing seems a lot more . . . I don't know. Shady. I tell myself it's just because I almost got caught today and my grades have been slipping, and that it has nothing to do with Cole and everything to do with me. I make a private vow to myself that I really *am* going to do better, cut down the amount of time I spend playing, make sure I'm home most nights, keep up with my schoolwork.

But by the time the salads arrive at our table, I still don't feel better. I push my lettuce around the plate.

"So tell me about your family," I say, mostly because I don't feel like talking about poker. "You never really talk about them." A look of surprise and something else (worry?) crosses Cole's face, but it's gone so fast that I think maybe I imagined it.

"Honestly, I don't think we should be worrying about meeting the parents just yet, Shannon Card." He gives me a grin, then dunks a piece of bread into his salad dressing and takes a big bite.

"I didn't mean—"

"It's okay," he says, holding up his hand. He leans across the table and motions me close. I rise a bit in my chair dutifully and lean toward him. "Do you want to know a secret?" he whispers in my ear.

"Always," I say.

"Me and you," he says, "are about to become very rich."

"That's not really a secret," I say. In fact, it's pretty much all we talk about.

He motions me closer. "That's just because you don't know the plan." His breath is on my ear, and I flash back to all the nights we've spent lying in his bed, kissing and . . . yeah. I take a deep breath and try to stop all the flipping that's going on in my stomach.

"What plan?" I ask.

"I'm going to tell you," he says. "Tonight."

And then he goes back to eating, like nothing is going on.

11

$\mathcal{I}$ figured we'd be going back to Cole's hotel room after dinner so that he could clue me in on his big plan, but in a move that makes no sense, he invites me over to his friend Logan's house. I'm confused, but since it's the first time I've been invited anywhere to meet any of Cole's friends, I jump at the chance.

"I can't stay out too late," I remind him as we walk up the steps to Logan's apartment. I called my mom to tell her I was going to be late, but I can't stay out too

too late. Since the whole thing happened with my parents freaking out, I have to get home early at least for a week or so.

"Yeah, I know," he says. "Shannon Card, you know how you're always bugging me to meet the other members of Aces Up?"

"Yes," I say. Actually, that's not *exactly* true. I used to bug him a lot, but I've come to realize that it's better not to bug him. He doesn't take kindly to bugging. Not that he gets mean or anything. He just ignores me.

Besides, eventually I started not to care about the other members of Aces. I have my hands full hanging out with Cole, and as long as I'm making money, I don't need a circle of poker-playing BFFs. In fact, I decided a little while ago that it's probably better if I don't have them. The fewer people who know about what I'm doing, the better.

"Well, get ready to meet them," he says.

He opens the door to the apartment, and there, in the living room, are two guys and a girl. The guys are sitting on an overstuffed green couch, playing a video game, and the girl is lounging sideways in the armchair, her long legs dangling over the side.

"You asshole!" one of the guys is saying. "You know that's an illegal move!"

"That move," the other guy says, "is not illegal. Just because I happen to know the secret code!" He stands up and does a little dance, like the kind really annoying football players do when they get a touchdown.

"Hey, Cole," the girl says. She's wearing a camou-flage baseball hat and matching camouflage cargo capris. She doesn't say anything to me, just goes back to staring up at the ceiling.

"Hey," Cole says. He pulls his leather jacket off and hangs it on the rack by the door. "This is Shannon."

"Hi," the guys chorus, their eyes never moving from the screen. They look familiar, maybe because I've seen them playing cards at the casino.

The girl still doesn't say anything. She just shifts on the chair. She looks familiar, too, probably because she looks like any stereotypical popular girl on any show on The CW. Cole walks into the kitchen, leaving me alone in the living room. *These* are the other members of Aces Up? Hmmm. Not too friendly, are they? Plus I figured they'd be older. And look like Mafia bosses or something. But they don't. They just look like . . . reg-ular college kids. But then again, so do I. Well. A reg-ular high school kid, at least.

I make my way over to another chair and sit down. Still no one talks to me.

"So what's the video game about?" I ask, deciding to try and be polite.

Obviously this is a foolish thing to ask, because Guy Number Two says, "It's Grand Mal Seizure," which doesn't really answer my question. From what I can tell, the game consists of the two of them beat-ing the crap out of each other, so maybe it's self-explanatory. Like they're trying to give each other grand mal seizures.

Cole returns from the kitchen, carrying a six-pack of beer, which he sets down on the table in front of everyone. I take one, mostly because I don't know what else to do with myself.

"Can we please turn that off?" he asks. "We need to get started."

One of the guys picks up the remote and turns off the TV.

"Did you guys introduce yourselves to Shannon?" Cole asks.

"We were just about to," Guy Number Two says, rolling his eyes. He's the one who knew the secret code. He's wearing a black zip-up hoodie and he has a hemp bracelet on his wrist. "I'm Joe," he says, giving me a mock salute.

"And I'm Logan," the other one says. He has blond spiky hair and a tattoo of a bar code on the back of his neck.

"Michelle," the girl says. She sits up in the chair and looks straight at Cole.

"And this," Cole says again, "is Shannon." This time he says it like I'm his best-kept secret or something, and it makes me blush a little.

"So you're the one who made that amazing call the other night," Joe says. He looks impressed.

"What call?" I ask, frowning.

"You called your two pair against a guy who was totally bluffing," Joe says. "Cole told me all about it." I frown. I remember the call and the hand he's talking about (it was a few nights ago, and I had three sixes and called when there were two aces on the board, because I just had a feeling), but I had no idea Cole was watching me.

"I'm ordering pizza," Michelle announces. She rolls her eyes. What? Why is she rolling her eyes? Is she . . . was she rolling her eyes about *my poker call*? That was a really great call! I narrow my eyes at her and watch as she gets up and grabs Cole's cell phone out of his jacket pocket. "What does everyone want?"

"Pepperoni," Logan says.

"Mushroom and sausage," Joe says. "And extra cheese."

"Everything on mine," Cole says. "Except pineapple."

Nobody asks me what I want. But whatever. I mean, I'm not really that hungry after just having been out to dinner. And besides, I'm sure I can just share with someone else. Cole, for sure, will share his pizza with me. Even though it seems like he's a little, uh, distracted right now.

"So," Cole says, "it's been decided that the five of us will be playing in the National Championship of Poker."

"Yes!" Logan says, pumping his fist.

"That's awesome," I say. Michelle looks at me with disgust. On hold with the pizza place, she has Cole's cell phone cradled against her shoulder. Why couldn't she use her own cell phone? If she's trying to prove that she's closer to him than I am, well, then that's just ridiculous. I mean, we were practically naked in each other's arms last night. I think that's a little better than using someone's dumb phone. And besides, who is she? If she was even remotely important to him, I would have heard about her.

Really? a little voice in my head says. Would you *really* have heard of her? But I push it away. I have way more important things to think about. Like the National Championship of Poker, which I'm now apparently going to be playing in! The National Championship of Poker is this huge tournament that happens once a year, and this year it's happening at the Collosio.

It costs ten thousand dollars to get in, but it's a winner-take-all, one-day tournament, and the grand prize can be millions, depending on how many entries they get. This year they're projecting the prize to be thirteen million dollars. THIRTEEN MILLION DOLLARS. Can you imagine what I could do with thirteen million dollars? I could definitely pay for Wellesley. I could get myself an off-campus apartment, which I've been dreaming about ever since the nightmare of having to share a dorm room with Parvati became a possibility. I could buy my parents a house and get Robyn tons of new shoes or any kind of clothes she wanted and pay her tuition to any school in the world.

"So what's the plan?" Joe asks. The TV has been turned back on, and a new game has been loaded into the Wii, and now he's playing some kind of sports game, moving his body all around. It looks like maybe aliens are trying to get him while he's playing basketball. I'm not exactly sure.

Cole gets up from the couch and turns off the game.

"Hey!" Logan protests. "We hadn't even saved that yet."

"Yeah, well, this is a little bit more important," Cole says.

"Totally important," Michelle says, shooting me a death glare. What is her *problem*? I'm completely listening.

"Are we sticking with the signaling and dumping idea?" Logan asks.

Cole lounges back on the couch and pulls a cigarette from the pack in front of him. "It's not an idea," he says. "And I don't want us underestimating how hard it's going to be, either."

"I wasn't," Logan says. He looks nervous. "I was just asking a question."

"Yeah, well, a little more listening, a little less asking." Wow. Cole's in a mood tonight. But I guess you have to be when you're in charge.

"Okay," Joe says. "We're listening."

"Yeah," Michelle says. "I'm listening." She pulls a lighter out of nowhere and reaches over to give Cole a light. He leans into her fingers, lights the cigarette, and then blows a ring of smoke lazily toward the ceiling.

"Thanks," Cole says, giving her a sexy smile. Hmmm.

"You're welcome," she says, beaming at the attention.

"Signaling and dumping what?" I ask.

Michelle rolls her eyes and doesn't answer me.

"So is it just going to be us?" Joe asks, also ignoring me. "Because if we're going to get JC and Carey involved, I think we should wait until we talk to them."

I wonder if Carey's nicer than Michelle.

"Not Carey," Cole says. "He has a big mouth, and he's even worse than Carter." Oh. So Carey's a boy. So much for girl bonding. "And JC is going to be in Vegas." He reaches over and taps his cigarette on the ashtray. Michelle reaches into the pack and lights up, too. I have nothing to do with my hands, so I settle for folding them in my lap. I feel like a little kid who's been allowed to sit at the grown-up table and is waiting for someone to let her in on the conversation.

"So what are we doing?" I ask, louder this time, trying my best to insert myself into the conversation.

"Fixing the tournament," Joe says. He must notice the look of confusion on my face, because he leans forward and says to Cole. "Shit, Cole. I thought you said she was cool."

"She is," Cole says. He moves to the other end of the couch, reaches over, and touches my knee. "Aren't you, Shannon Card?"

"Oh, yeah," I say. "I'm cool." They can't *really* be talking about fixing the tournament, can they? I mean, that's ridiculous. First of all, you can't just *fix* a tournament. You need corrupt dealers or someone on the inside. That's what always happens in the movies, anyway—the cops are always going on and on, trying to figure out who the perps were working with on the inside.

"So we'll all be entering," Cole says. "And it's going to be a rough couple of weeks, getting the signals down, and figuring out how to dump." Everyone's looking at him seriously now, and he seems to relish being in the spotlight. He looks at each of us carefully. "It's going to be hard work, and I don't want anyone taking anything for granted."

"Wait," I say dumbly. "Are you guys really talking about fixing the tournament?"

"Well, not exactly," Cole says. He's still rubbing my knee. "It's impossible to fix the tournament unless you have someone working for you on the inside." Aha! I knew it. I shoot Michelle a triumphant look, even though she can't possibly know that's what I was thinking. Plus chances are she already knew that part about the inside.

"But you can give yourself the best chance," Cole says. "You can bend the odds in your favor."

"How?" I ask.

"By dumping chips to one person," Logan says. "And by signaling to each other what you have."

"And even then," Cole says, "we have to keep our wits about us and make sure we last until we all end up at the same table. And there will be other people there, other people who are working with us, although we think it's best that you don't know who those people are until later."

I'm starting to get it. By using a system of signaling to each other to tell each other what cards we have, we'll be better able to figure out what might come on the board and whether we should fold or stay in the hand. If we're playing at the same table (which probably won't happen until later on in the tournament), we'll lose on purpose and dump all our chips to one person so that person has a good chance of winning. And then we'll all split the money at the end.

"So wait," I say. "How many people are going to be playing from Aces Up?"

"Don't worry, Shannon Card," Cole says. "If one of us wins the grand prize, you'll be guaranteed at least fifty grand."

Fifty grand? Um, that's great and everything (don't get me wrong, fifty grand is amazing, actually), but when you put that up against the fact that the grand prize is thirteen million dollars, it seems a little paltry. What happened to "I have a secret. Me and you are going to be very rich"?

"Actually," I say, "if you don't mind, I think I'd like to take my chances by myself."

They all stare at me.

"Shannon, you can't just pick and choose when you want to be in Aces," Cole says. "We're paying your way into the tournament, so you're either in or you're out."

"Oh," I say. "Sorry, then I'm in. Definitely in." He visibly relaxes, and everyone starts talking and semi-arguing about who would be the best person to dump the chips to. And then I realize why I've never met any of the other members before now. It's easier for them to get away with cheating if they're not seen together—that way, no one can really prove they're all connected and working together.

A cold feeling of dread rises inside me.

"Um, Cole," I say, "can I talk to you for a second?"

"Of course," he says. He reaches out and rubs my leg again, only this time it feels a little . . . wrong. He's looking at me expectantly, and I realize he wants me to talk in front of everyone.

"Uh," I say. "Can we go outside for a second?"

"Sure." He grins.

Once the door is shut behind us and we're out in the hall, he pulls me close to him, and for a second, I almost convince myself that everything might be okay.

"Listen," I say into the softness of his sweatshirt, "I really think we should do this on our own. Think about the millions we could make."

"Shannon," Cole says, stroking my hair, "you're not ready."

"Maybe not," I say. "But I want to try. I'm getting better, and *you're* definitely ready."

"That's not what's been decided," he says simply.

I pull away and look at him. "Not what's been

decided?" I ask incredulously. "What are you, a pod person?"

"No," he says. "I'm a member of Aces Up, which is also what you're supposed to be."

"I am," I say. "I just . . . I'm not sure if it makes the most sense. Fifty thousand dollars? That's really not that much money."

"It's almost one whole year of school," he says. "Without financial aid." He pulls me close again and says, "It's cute the way you ask so many questions. But honestly, Shannon Card, you need to just relax and trust me."

I know he's trying to make me feel better, and usually I find his whole mysterious vibe kind of sexy. But this time, it just seems . . . well, a little creepy.

"So are you in?" Cole asks. I hesitate for a second, because honestly, I'm not sure. And then, before I can stop him, Cole opens the door and steps back into the apartment. "Call me when you decide." He closes the door, leaving me out in the hall.

♥ ♠ ♣ ♦

Well. I guess it's to be expected. I mean, all couples go through growing pains, right? It's inevitable. Still. Usually those fights happen because the guy doesn't want to commit, or there've been some sketchy pictures or comments on someone's Facebook page. Not because your boyfriend wants to fix one of the biggest poker tournaments in the world and you're trying to convince him not to. What is wrong with him, anyway? I think as I drive home.

I mean, besides it being totally and completely wrong, what if we get caught? They have cameras all over the casino. During my orientation, I had to watch a bunch of videos that basically conveyed the message "YOU WILL NEVER GET AWAY WITH CHEATING SO DON'T EVEN TRY IT OR YOU WILL BE JAILED." There was this very sad-looking man shaking his head and saying, "I don't know why I did it! I ruined my life, and I lost my job and my friends." Then it showed a bunch of casino employees hanging out and having fun, and of course Sad Guy couldn't join in anymore, because he wasn't there and was basically dead to all his friends.

If Aces Up gets caught . . . Actually, screw that, if *I* get caught, I won't be allowed into Wellesley. I might go to jail. I might have a criminal record! My parents would have to come bail me out. Or maybe they'd just leave me in jail, since by the time I got a trial, I'd probably be eighteen. Can you imagine? Me, in jail for gambling fraud? I'm so caught up in figuring out the legal penalties for what Aces Up is talking about doing that when I get home, at first I don't realize that every single light in the house is on.

And it takes me a while to process the fact that everyone in my family is awake when I open the door and find them all in the kitchen, staring at me.

"Oh, God," I say when I see the stricken look on my mom's face. "What happened?" Someone died. I just know it. Thank God I see Robyn and my dad there; otherwise I might just have assumed it was one of them. "Is it . . . is it Grandma Card?" I whisper.

My grandma Card is not in the best of health. Physically she's okay, but mentally she gets a little sketchy. Like she ends up walking around in the street with her bathrobe on or calls up and orders lots of things from infomercials and then gets confused and accuses someone of taking her credit card when the things arrive.

"Shannon," my mom says, "I think you should sit down." And then I see my sister's face. She's standing up, leaning against the fridge, her arms crossed and her long hair hanging down, hiding her face. And then I know. She told them. That I've been staying out all night, that she thinks I was lying about being at Mackenzie's, and that Leonardo saw me at the casino.

"You *told* them?" I demand. I wait for her to look up and say, "Told them what? I don't know what you're talking about. This is a meeting about the family finances," or something like that, but all she does is look up at me and bite her lip.

"I'm sorry," she says. "But they found out you weren't at the Rusty Nail, and they . . . Shannon, I was worried."

Worried! She was *worried*? I can't freakin' believe this. All those times she snuck out in the middle of the night to go meet Leonardo, all those times she came home drunk and I kept my mom from going into her room . . . And now Robyn was *worried,* and so she told on me?

Okay. I can't let myself start getting caught up in that kind of thinking. It will do nothing but get me rattled, and besides, there will be plenty of time for revenge scenarios later. Still. I feel like screaming.

"Do you want to tell us what's going on?" my dad asks.

"Can I have some tea first?" I ask, stalling. How the hell did everything become such a complete and total mess in the span of just a few hours?

My dad gets up from the table and starts to fill the teakettle. "Talk while it heats," he commands. So much for stalling.

I look at my mom and give her a tentative smile, but she doesn't return it. She's been silent, which is actually kind of scary. Yelling would definitely be better. Then I could yell back, and we could have it all out and then make up.

"Well," I say, "as I suppose you must have figured out because of information supplied by Robyn"—I shoot a pointed look at my sister—"I haven't been working at the Rusty Nail."

"And where have you been working?" my mom asks. Her voice is very . . . steely.

"Weeell," I say. "I have been waitressing, just not at the Rusty Nail."

"And where *have* you been waitressing?" my mom wants to know.

"Um, well," I say, "I've been waitressing at the Collosio." I deliberately leave out the casino part, because

200

I really don't think that's very relevant. My dad has set the teakettle on the burner and is standing with his arms crossed. It's very quiet in the kitchen, which feels all wrong given the fact that I'm in trouble and therefore should be getting yelled at.

"Shannon, you have to be twenty-one to work there," my mom says.

"Well, yes, *technically*," I say. "But you guys have always taught me not to let obstacles stand in the way of my dreams." This is totally true. In fact, when I told my mom that Parvati was going to win the math award because she was smarter than me, my mom told me that wasn't true and I just needed to work harder. Kind of ironic that I didn't take her advice then and am now going to lose out on the math award, while her advice came in quite handy when it came to getting an illegal job.

"Not letting obstacles stand in the way of your dreams is far different than doing something that's illegal," my mom says. My dad and my sister are still quiet. "Getting a job that you're too young for is one thing. Gambling is quite another."

"I'm not gambling!" The lie slips out easily, before I can even think about it. "Robyn," I demand, "what did you tell them?"

"The truth," Robyn says. "That Leonardo saw you at the casino, late at night and on several occasions, all dressed up, and playing poker." She sounds like a police report. My mouth drops open in shock.

"You're going to believe Leonardo over me?" I ask my dad. "After all he's done to you?" Leonardo really hasn't done that much to my dad except annoy him, but still. Taking Leonardo's word over his own daughter's is completely unacceptable.

My dad stays silent. The teakettle chooses that moment to go off, so he reaches over the stove and pulls down a mug, drops a teabag into it, and fills it with steaming water. He sets it in front of me, and I wrap my fingers around it, letting the warmth fill my hands.

"Look," I say, deciding to go for the truth, or at least part of it, "I'm sorry I lied to you guys about the job. But you know that I got into Wellesley. And there's no way we can afford it. I was being proactive. I was taking control of *my own destiny*."

"You lied," my mom says simply. "You lied to us about where you were and what you were doing, and then you stayed out all night gambling."

"I wasn't gambling," I say. "Poker is a skill-based game." I decide it's probably best not to mention that any money I used was given to me by Aces Up. I don't think my parents would see that as a positive. I take a sip of my tea, and it's bitter on my tongue, because with all the drama, I forgot to add sugar. I reach for the bowl in the middle of the table and dump three heaping spoonfuls in.

"It's gambling," my mom says. "And you lied."

"It's pretty much the same as playing the stock market," I say, going for my ace in the hole. I try to make my voice sound bright, but my hand is shaking as I return the teaspoon to the sugar bowl. "Isn't that what you always say, Dad? That the stock market is pretty much one big gamble."

"It's not the same," my dad says. "And you're underage."

I look sulkily into my tea. My eyes fill up with tears, and I blink them back. Suddenly, I feel totally humiliated. My parents are acting like I'm some kind of delinquent. And I haven't seen my dad this quiet and depressed-looking since the day he lost his job. I try to force a smile onto my face, but a little voice in the back of my head is starting to speak up. And that voice is saying that maybe this wasn't such a good idea. That it's great to try and make money for school, but maybe I'm a little bit too deep into this, and maybe my parents are right.

I mean, let's recap, shall we?

I have used a fake ID and a fake birth certificate to get a job in a casino, which is illegal and pretty shady.

I know nothing, really, about the guy I am hooking up with.

Said guy just told me that he is going to fix a poker tournament. *Fix* it! Like *cheat*.

And then I start to get mad. Really, really mad. My parents are the ones who put me in this situation. You'd think that they'd have set up a nice, no-risk college fund for me when they had the chance. I know they should have, because at one point after my dad lost his job, I heard him say, "We should have put our money into a nice, no-risk college fund." People do it. They take a few thousand dollars and put it into an account and add like fifty bucks a month for twenty years, and it turns into enough for you to pay for college. I learned about it in social studies in seventh grade.

"Well," I say, my fists tightening around my tea mug, "maybe I wouldn't be in this situation if some people had been a little more careful with their money." It comes out even sharper than I intended it, and my dad looks like he's been slapped. For a second, I want to take it back, but I don't. I *can't*.

I cross my arms and look at my mom. "So what's my punishment?" I ask.

"You're grounded," my mom says simply. My dad looks at the floor, and my sister does the same. "And you're to quit your job immediately."

"Quit my job?" I screech. "What am I supposed to do for money?"

"You have permission to look for another job," my mom says. "But you are not to return to the casino under any circumstances." I don't say anything.

And then my mom walks out of the kitchen, and my dad and my sister file out behind her.

When I get up to my room, my hands are shaking so bad that it takes forever to unbutton the shirt I'm wearing and change into a pair of pajama pants and a T-shirt. Okay, I tell myself, just calm down. Think. All I need is a plan.

Step one, call Cole and try to talk him out of this ridiculous idea to fix the tournament. Step two, figure out a way to play in the tournament and win so that I can pay for Wellesley. Step three, quit. And when I say quit, I mean everything—Aces Up, playing poker, and the waitressing job. Although the job is probably going to have to go ASAP. Adrienne is not going to be too happy about me not giving her any notice, but I guess in the long run it will be better, since even though she won't know it, she won't be risking getting in trouble for employing a minor.

I'll get my grades back up. I'll work really hard on my math. And once my parents see that I'm not two seconds away from falling into the seedy underground world of gambling and debauchery, everything will be back to normal.

I dial Cole's number, feeling like maybe this just might work.

"Yeah?" he answers. There are a lot of voices in the background, and I can hear Michelle giggling. Ugh.

"Hey," I say. "It's me."

"Hi," he says. He doesn't sound too friendly or happy to hear from me. You'd think he would be, since we just had our first official fight.

"Um, what are you doing?"

"Talking," he says. In the background, a girl squeals, *"Stop doing that with the chicken wings!"* and then there's a huge round of laughter. Laughter that includes female voices.

"With who?" I ask, hoping it sounds like I want to know who he's talking to, when I really want to know what girls are over.

"Everyone," he says.

"Well, um," I say, "I was just calling because I wanted to make sure we were cool, you know, and not in a fight."

"We're not in a fight," he says.

"Oh, good," I say, relief flooding through my body. I lean back on my bed and snuggle into my body pillow. "Because I didn't want us to—"

"I don't fight with people," Cole says. "Grudges aren't my thing."

"Oh." All right then. Grudges aren't his thing? What's that supposed to mean? "So we're cool, then?" I ask.

"We're cool," Cole says. "As long as you're going to do the right thing." His tone is cold and scary, and I don't have to ask him what he means by "do the right thing." It means going along with their crazy plan. And I can tell he means that if I don't, we're over. And who knows what else. Suddenly, I feel scared. Like really, really scared.

"Yes," I whisper, "I'm going to do the right thing."

"Good," he says. "I'll call you later, Shannon Card." He disconnects without saying goodbye, and I stare at the phone for a second. Okay, Shannon. Think. Who can I call to talk about this? Robyn, who is my usual confidante in all things, is out of the question for obvious reasons.

So I dial Mackenzie.

"Hello?" she says. "It's about time!"

"What do you mean, 'it's about time'?" I ask.

"I thought you were going to call me as soon as you told her, see what she said," Mackenzie says. "Did she freak out?"

I have no idea what she's talking about. Did who freak out? My mom? Does Mackenzie know my secrets? And then I remember. Adrienne. Mackenzie was going to call in to work tonight so that she could hang out with Filipe. But she wanted *me* to tell Adrienne, since she said she's horrible at getting people to believe that she's really sick. Technically, there's no rule that you have to call in yourself, so Mackenzie figured I could do it, since I was going to be at work anyway. But I completely forgot.

"Oh, no," I say, my stomach dropping. "Don't kill me."

"Why would I kill you?" Mackenzie asks. "If she was mad, it's not your fault." Filipe says something to her in the background that I can't quite make out, and Mackenzie giggles.

"Well, she wasn't mad," I say. "But that's because I forgot to tell her."

There's a pause on the other end, and then Mackenzie bursts out laughing. "Oh my God, Shannon," she says. "For a second I totally thought you were being serious."

"I'm so, *so* sorry," I say. "I'll call her right now, I'll leave her a voice mail on her cell and at work, I'll tell her that it's my fault, I'll totally take care of it, I promise."

Silence. Then "Didn't you notice that I wasn't at work? How could you *forget* something like that?"

Because I was all caught up in Cole, and some big illegal gambling operation, and my parents, and Max, and math, and I'm a horrible friend and I didn't think about it?

"I don't know," I whisper.

"Whatever," Mackenzie says. "You know, lately you've been acting really selfish." And then she hangs up. I stare at the phone in shock. She hung up on me! The second person in as many minutes to hang up on me! And my family did the equivalent by walking out of the kitchen, so she's kind of the fifth.

If that many people are hanging up on you in that many minutes, especially your friends and your parents and your sister, something is definitely wrong.

I feel tears starting to prick at my eyes. How did everything get so complicated? Just a few months ago, I was meandering along, trying to beat out Parvati for the math scholarship, secretly lusting after Max, heartbroken but drama free, and just living my life. Now all of a sudden everything is a big mess. My parents hate me, Robyn hates me, Mackenzie hates me, Max hates me, and Cole wants me to do something that at best is completely and totally morally wrong, and at worst could send me to jail.

Before I can stop myself, I'm picking my phone up and scrolling through until I find Max's number. On the fourth ring, I realize he's not going to answer, which is fine, because honestly, what would I say? I guess I can just leave a message telling him that I'm sorry about the tutoring thing not working out, and that I wish him the best. That's okay, right? Although I don't know why I would be calling him in the middle of the night to say that. It doesn't make much sense. Or I could just say, "Oh, sorry, I must have dialed the wrong number in my phone. I was trying to reach my boyfriend," but again, that seems a little unbelievable. Maybe I'll just hang up and leave him wondering why I would call him so late at night and if maybe—

"Hello?" His voice sounds scratchy but not sleepy, like maybe he's on the computer or watching TV and just hasn't spoken in a while. I picture him all rumpled in a sweatshirt, and my heart jumps into my throat, and I can't talk. "Shannon?" he says just as I'm about to hang up the phone. Curse you, caller ID!

"Oh," I say. "Hey. Um, I thought you'd be sleeping."

"Then why did you call me?" He sounds amused, maybe even a little bit happy to hear from me, which is a change from the last time I talked to him and from the other people I've been coming into contact with tonight.

"I was going to leave you a message," I say.

"So you didn't want to talk to me?"

"No," I say. "Yes, I mean, I did want to talk to you, but when you didn't answer right away, I thought I'd leave a message." I pull at a stray thread that's popped out of the lining of my pillowcase, wrapping it around my finger.

"What was the message going to say?"

"I dunno," I say. "I figured I had one or two more rings to figure out something cute."

"You wanted me to think you were cute?"

No. Yes. "I don't know."

"Are we in a fight?" he asks me.

"Yes," I say. "We're in a fight."

"So are you calling to work it out?"

"I don't know," I say. "Because I'm not even exactly sure what we're fighting about."

"A lot of things," he says. "Kisses, gambling, your boyfriend, what happened over the summer, what a total jerk I am . . ." He trails off, and I don't say anything. My heart aches, because suddenly, I miss him so much. Not just him, physically, but how we used to be, how I could tell him everything and he would understand, how I could call him anytime, day or night, and he would be there. It hurts so much it makes my whole chest ache. "Speaking of your boyfriend . . . ," he says. "Would he approve of such a late-night phone call?"

"I'm not sure," I say. "We're kind of in a fight, too."

"About what?" he asks.

"It's . . . complicated," I say. And then I have an idea. "What are you doing right now?"

"I'm involved in a very spirited online video game tournament with Chris Harmon," he says.

"Oh," I say. "No, I understand. I just . . . My sleep schedule is all screwed up lately, so sometimes I really feel like hanging out with someone, you know, late at night, and all my other friends are busy or sleeping, you know, like normal people, so I just thought—"

"Shannon," Max says, cutting me off.

"Yeah?"

"I was kidding."

"You're not playing online video games?"

"Oh, no, I am," he says. "But it's not something I can't get out of." There's a pause, and I hold my breath. "Wanna meet me at IHOP?" he asks. "Twenty minutes?"

I think about the fact that I'm grounded, and that sneaking out is most definitely not the best idea. And then I think about Max, and how badly I want to see him.

"Sure," I say, hoping I sound calmer than I feel.

13

When I get to IHOP, Max is already there, sitting in a booth and sipping some coffee. He looks up as I approach him.

"Hey," he says.

"Hi," I say, suddenly feeling awkward as I slide into the booth.

"I waited for you to order," Max says, sliding the menu across the table to me. And I don't know why—maybe it's because that was a really thoughtful thing to do, or maybe it's because I'm so emotional, or maybe it's because I still really do miss him—but the next thing I know, I burst into tears.

Max looks shocked for a second but recovers quickly. "Whoa, whoa, whoa," he says. He gets up and slides into my side of the booth. He puts his arms around me, and I cry into his shirt, my tears leaving little tracks on his jacket.

"You must think I'm so stupid," I say. He hands me a napkin and I blow my nose. "Yelling at you in the library, and then calling you and now . . . now . . ." I'm crying too hard to finish.

"I don't think you're stupid," Max says, pushing my hair out of my face.

The waitress, who obviously isn't paying attention to the fact that there is a complete and total mental breakdown going on in our booth, comes over and asks us what we want to order. "We need a minute," Max tells her. "We'll let you know when we're ready."

"No," I say, sitting up and brushing my tears away with another napkin. "I know what I want. Chocolate cake."

"And some hash browns to share?" Max asks hopefully.

"No," I say. "French fries with gravy."

He grins. "And another coffee." The waitress writes down our order and then leaves.

"You okay?" Max asks.

"Yeah," I say, blowing my nose one more time. Ugh. So gross. Max returns to his side of the booth, and for a second I consider asking him to stay on my side, but I don't.

"Listen, I'm sorry about being such a jerk to you before," I say. "When you wanted to talk, I mean. It was just a lot to deal with, with the kissing stuff and Parvati and . . ."

"I'm sorry, too," Max says. "You playing poker is really none of my business. And I'm sorry I told Ms. Kellogg that you quit tutoring me. That wasn't right of me, because honestly, it was both of our faults."

"No," I say, sighing. "It was *my* fault. You tried to talk to me, and I kept blowing you off." Looking back, I realize that was pretty crappy of me. Max was trying to talk to me, and I just ignored him. "Besides, I shouldn't have . . . you know, tried to, uh, kiss you." My face is burning, and I hope he can't see how totally and completely embarrassing this is for me.

"Whatever," Max says. "It's not really important."

It isn't? "It isn't?"

"No," he says, looking at me. He's balling his straw wrapper up in his hands and twirling it around his fingers. "What's important is the reason I blew you off over the summer."

I hold my breath.

"Shannon, I'm sorry," he says. He reaches across the table and grabs my hands, and electricity shoots up my arms. "I just . . . I freaked out. We were friends and I got scared and I didn't really know how to deal with it."

For a second, anger wells up inside me, but then it

burns itself out. "You could have called me, we could have talked. It didn't have to be this big thing." But of course it *was* a big thing.

"I know that now," he says. "But I cared about you so much, you were the only thing I had in my life that I felt was so real and so good, and then I thought, Oh, God, what's going to happen if we mess this all up with kissing and stuff? and I freaked out." He looks down at the table. "I just needed some time to think about it. But then somehow I lost you altogether, and I didn't know how to get you back."

There's a lump in my throat, and I try to speak around it, but the words won't come.

"Anyway," he says, releasing my hands, "it doesn't matter now."

"It doesn't?" I ask.

"No," he says. "Because you have a boyfriend."

"Oh," I say. "Right." I consider mentioning that Cole isn't technically my boyfriend, but then decide not to, because I'm not ready to go there.

The food comes and we talk about school and people we know and sports and everything else. And he tells me about the Parvati breakup, about how they had been growing apart and how she's already dating some other guy.

And it's fun just to talk. For the first time in a while, I'm not running through different combos of cards in my head or nodding off in English class or worrying that my parents are going to go upstairs and find my bed empty. (Well, I'm a little worried about that last one, because I *did* sneak out of the house.) I'm not nervous about whether I'll be able to find Cole at the end of the night, or whether Adrienne is going to march up and fire me because she knows I'm lying about my age. I'm just me. And it feels good. And relaxing. And real.

When the waitress comes to check on us, I order a black-and-white milk shake, and Max looks impressed and then orders the same thing.

"I forgot," he says, "what a great orderer you are. Most girls do not know how to order."

I blush.

"So," he says. "Is it serious?" He looks up at me from under his eyelashes and I remember how close we were that night at the party and I have the inexplicable urge to go to the other side of the booth and slide in next to him.

"Is what serious?" I ask.

"The thing with this guy," he says. "Your relationship, is it serious?"

"No," I say, looking him straight in the eye. "And after tonight, it's even less serious."

"Oh?" he says. I can see the hope in his eyes, and I think he might think that it's because of him. And partly it is, but it's also partly because of all the other stuff.

"We, uh, had a weird night," I say. And then I tell Max everything. About Adrienne, about Mackenzie's being mad at me, about Aces Up, about Cole's only wanting to make out with me in his room (which is actually pretty embarrassing to say out loud, but Max is totally sympathetic and gets that "oh my God, I can't believe what scumbags guys can be, even though I am a guy" look on his face), and about what he's trying to do with the tournament. When I tell him that, Max seems shocked. "So what are you going to do?" he asks.

"I dunno," I say, squirming around in my seat. "I mean, I've never actually been in this situation. And really, is it that bad? What they're doing, I mean?" Of course, I already know what he's going to say.

"Um, yeah."

I let out a huge sigh, because I know he's right. "I know," I say. "I know it is. But what can I do? If I don't go along with it . . . at best, they'll turn me in for being underage. At worst, well . . . I don't know. Not to mention that I'm already in so much trouble with my parents, and they don't even know the worst part of it."

He looks at me. And then he gets really serious and lowers his voice. "So beat them," he says.

"Beat them?" I look at him incredulously. "What do you mean, 'beat them'?"

"Beat them all," he says. "Just enter the tournament yourself, and don't go along with their dumb signaling or whatever, and just . . . you know, beat them."

"Oh, Max," I say, looking at him fondly. "You obviously aren't that much into the poker thing."

"You mean I don't get it?"

"Yes," I say. "You don't get it." The waitress comes back with our milk shakes, and I take a big sip and let the coldness spread through my body. So. Good.

"Maybe I don't," Max says. "But I do know that one time I saw Chris sit down at a table and win five hundred bucks off some guy in about fifteen minutes. And if Chris Harmon can do that, then you can definitely beat some dumb college kids."

"Except," I say, "they're not just some dumb college kids. They're the best poker players around."

"Around where?" he asks, looking skeptical.

"You know, around," I say. "It's metaphorical." I take another sip of my shake.

"If they're so good," he says, "then why aren't they in Vegas?"

"Because they go to school here," I say.

"If they're so good," he says, "then why do they have to go to school?"

"Because," I say. "They want to?" He raises his eyebrows at me again.

"Stop looking at me with skeptical eyebrows," I say.

"Look, you're giving them too much credit," he says. "You're looking at them the way they present themselves, instead of the way they really are."

"So you think they're pulling the wool over my eyes?" I say, a little interested. It definitely could be true. I mean, besides the times we played in Cole's bedroom and the times he sat at my table, I haven't really even seen him play. And I've never seen him in a tournament. I don't really know how good of a poker player he is—I only think he's great because he told me he is.

"Yes," Max says. He leans forward in the booth and looks right into my eyes. "And I know you can beat them."

"But even if I *could*," I say, "it's not going to matter. I told you, if I don't go along with their plan, they'll definitely turn me in for being underage. Especially if I let them buy my way in."

"How much does it cost?" he asks.

"Ten thousand dollars," I say.

Max's jaw drops. I kind of like impressing him. It gives me cred. "Do you have that much?" he asks. "To enter on your own?"

"Uh, no," I say. "Actually, that's not true. I have *almost* that much, and *maybe* I could have it by the time the tournament starts in two weeks. But I need that money for school."

"Then you have to go along with it," Max says seriously. "One tournament. Go along with it, and then get out."

"But if I get caught, I could get in a lot of trouble," I say. The whole situation is so hopeless that I almost start crying again.

Max comes over to my side of the table and puts his arms around me. "So make sure you don't get caught."

♥ ♠ ♣ ♦

Okay. New plan. Pretend to go along with what Aces Up is doing, but don't actually cheat. That way, if *they* get caught, I can just be like, "Oh, I wasn't involved." This will take a little bit of finagling on my part—trying to get knocked out of the tournament as quickly as possible, pretending to have forgotten the signals, etc. But I can do it.

I can *totally* do it. I can call Cole and convince him that I'm on board with the plan. I'm not that bad of an actress. In seventh grade I even got a callback for *You're a Good Man, Charlie Brown*. So he probably won't be able to tell I'm lying.

Still, though.

I don't call Cole when I leave the IHOP, like I told Max I would.

I don't call him when I get home.

I don't call him the next morning before school.

And by the time I'm in the library, trying to cram for a social studies test before first period, I still haven't called him. PHONE CALL FAIL.

"Did you call him yet?" Max asks, popping up behind me.

I scream and drop my history book onto the floor. Two random people sitting at a table across from me shoot me a dirty look.

"Don't," I say, "sneak up on me like that. Don't you know that I could be offed at any moment for messing with the most powerful poker society in the world?"

"I forgot," Max says. He lowers his voice. "Should

I talk in some kind of code, perhaps?" He's wearing a black sweater and jeans, and his hair is wet from the shower, like it is most mornings.

"Maybe," I say, picking up my backpack. "They may have bugged my bag or something." I look suspiciously at the kids who shushed me. "Or they might have spies." It feels nice to joke around about it a little bit.

"Answer my question," Max says. He pulls out the chair next to me and slides into it. His leg brushes against mine, and I pull away, not because I want to, but because it suddenly feels like my leg is on fire.

"No," I say. "I haven't called."

Max reaches into my bag and pulls out my phone. "Call," he says.

"I'm scared," I whine. "What if he—" Max puts his finger up to my lips, and my pulse starts racing about a million miles a minute.

"Fine," I say, mostly to distract myself from the reaction I'm having to his closeness. I take the cell phone out of his hands, and our fingers touch. Ahh! With all the touching, it's a good thing I'm pretty much done with Cole. Or about to be. Even though we're not officially broken up, I'm ninety-nine percent sure that lying to the guy you've been making out with, taking ten thousand dollars from him, and tricking him into thinking you're going to go along with his crazy scheme to fix the National Championship of Poker constitute a breakup of sorts.

I dial the number, my fingers shaking. Actually, they're not shaking as much as they could be, because (Max doesn't know this) there's no way that Cole is going to be awake this early. I mean, it's not even eight o'clock yet. Cole is a night owl. He likes to stay up late, playing poker, making plans, and partying the night away. And making out with me, although I guess that might change now. Will I still have to kiss him? Do I have to wait until after the tournament to break up with him? Do I have to be his, like, fake girlfriend? The thought makes my stomach turn. That would be *so*—

"Hello?" What is up with people answering their phones when they should be sleeping or out? Seriously, doesn't anyone ever screen anymore?

"Hey," I say. "It's me."

"Oh," he says. Wow. Totally unfriendly.

"Anyway, I wanted to, uh, say sorry again for what happened yesterday." I wait for him to say that he's sorry, too, but he doesn't. And then I hear voices in the background. Is he . . . Could Cole actually be in class? Or at the library studying? That would be a first. And then it hits me. Cole's up so early because he never went to sleep. He stayed up all night having fun, not even caring about me or what I was doing! And granted, it's not like I was at home crying into my pillow or anything, but he doesn't know that. What a jerk.

But then Cole switches gears.

"Me too," he says, his voice getting low. "I didn't

mean to upset you, and I should have talked to you before I sprang everything on you like that." He sighs, and if I didn't know better, I'd think he really was sorry. "Are you gonna come over tonight, Shannon Card?" he asks, his voice hopeful.

"Uh, I don't know," I say. "I'm kind of in trouble with my parents."

"I hope you can," he says. "We need to talk more about everything."

"Okay," I say uncertainly. Max is looking at me, making hand motions like I should keep going, keep talking, but I'm starting to get rattled. So much for my great acting skills. "And I want you to know that I'm totally on board. With everything. In fact, I'm excited."

"Awesome," Cole says. "And, Shannon?" His voice sounds all smoky.

"Yes?" I whisper.

"I miss you." He hangs up the phone before I have a chance to answer. And thank goodness, too, because hello? How am I supposed to respond to that with Max sitting right next to me?

"So?" Max demands as I close my cell phone and slide it back into my bag. "What's going on? What did he say?"

"He said, uh . . . he said that he wants to get together and talk."

"Talk?" Again with the skeptical eyebrows.

"Yes," I say, more firmly. "Talk." There's nothing wrong with talking. Talking is perfectly fine. Talking is what people do every single day.

"So basically he wants to make sure you're really in," Max sighs.

"Yes," I say. "He's going to try to sweet-talk me, but whatever. I mean, I told him I'm going along with it, and so I'm going to have to let him think that he's completely won me over, and that I'll do whatever he wants."

"Riiight," Max says. "Except that you have to make sure that he doesn't win you over, and *actually* get you to go along with it."

"Max!" I say, shocked. "Do you really think I'm that weak? That he could get me to go along with his dumb cheating plan?"

"Do *you* think you're that weak?"

"Well, he did say that he missed me," I say, just to mess with him a little.

Max thunks his head down on the table in front of him.

"Mmmhmm," he says. "I knew it. He's totally trying to play you."

"But I'm not going to fall for it!" I say. "Seriously, I'm not! I'm scared of him now. I'm afraid he might be a super-psycho killer—there's no way I'm going to be pulled in by him. If anything, I'm afraid of being alone with him. I just have to make him think everything's okay for a little while."

Max looks at me seriously. "Does that mean you have to still hook up with him?"

"I'm not sure," I say, looking at the floor. Neither one of us says anything for a minute.

"Do you want me to go with you when you have to see him?" Max finally asks, breaking the silence. "I could wait for you outside the casino or something, make sure he doesn't see us together."

"Too risky," I say. "Besides, I have tremendous willpower."

"You do?"

"Totally," I say. And then I look him right in the eye. "I'm somehow able to keep myself from kissing you, aren't I?" The bell rings, so I calmly gather my stuff and head out of the library.

♥ ♠ ♣ ♦

Ohmigod. I can't believe I said that. I mean, where did *that* come from? Am I a vixen? Am I some kind of flirtatious goddess and I didn't even know it? Probably not. More likely it was just sort of lucky. I mean, the bell rang at exactly the right time; otherwise it probably would have been pretty awkward. This way, I was able to scoop up all my stuff and get out of there without having to talk about it. In fact, I can just kind of pretend that it didn't happen.

Except when Parvati saunters up to my desk in math.

"Oh," I say. "Um, hi." Max isn't in the classroom yet. (Maybe he's back at the library, fanning himself before he can see me in math—either that or he had to, you know, stop at his locker.)

"I saw you and Max in the library," Parvati says. "And I'm not going to lie, Shannon, it didn't look good." She twirls a strand of hair around her finger and looks a little sad. "You guys were getting really cozy." The Parvati who had a breakdown has gone back to wherever she came from, and the old Parvati is back. "I mean, I don't want to believe it, but . . . I don't know, what would you think if you saw what I saw?"

"Uh," I say. "I mean, we *were* in the library, but we weren't, uh, getting cozy." I open my math book and pretend I'm working on some problems so that she'll go away. But she doesn't.

"It *looked* cozy," she says, and I'm afraid that Crazy Parvati is going to start to come out.

"It wasn't," I say.

"That's what it *looked like,*" she says.

"It *wasn't,*" I repeat. For some reason I can't come up with anything better, and I guess I'm kind of hoping that if I keep saying it, she'll believe me.

"Well, it looked cozy," she says again. Apparently Parvati is using the same technique I am. I see Max come into the classroom out of the corner of my eye, and when he sees me talking to Parvati, his eyes widen and he keeps walking to his seat.

"See?" I say. "Do you really think that if we were being all cozy, he would have just headed to his seat without even talking to me?"

"Obviously," she says, "since I'm standing here talking to you, and I am the person from whom the coziness should be kept." She holds out her hand. "Give me your phone," she demands.

"What?" I'm sure I've misheard her. "I'm sure I've misheard you."

"No, you didn't," she says. "Let me just look in your phone."

"I'm not giving you my phone!" I say. "Why would I do something like that?"

"So that I can check to see if there are any calls between you and Max." She crosses her arms and taps her foot.

"That's not any of your business," I say. "And even if it *was,* I would not give you my phone, because right now you are acting like a crazy person and who knows what you would do with it?"

"But we're friends," Parvati says. She looks shocked. "And friends don't keep secrets from each other." I want to tell her that we're not really friends, but Parvati's already on her way back to her seat, yelling over her shoulder, "You know, I thought you'd changed after you lent me your iPod."

And so then of course I start to feel a little bad. Because we *did* kind of girl bond in the hall that day. And I did just lie to her. And even though I know that there's absolutely nothing romantic going on between me and Max, I still feel a little bad.

I feel bad all during math, and I'm actually thinking that maybe I'll try to talk to Parvati after class and apologize. But then, a few minutes before the bell rings, Ms. Kellogg stands up and looks at everyone.

"Class," she says, "I have a special announcement to make."

We all turn to look at her, and I pray that she's not going to announce that we're having another pop quiz. I am so not up for that.

"The recipient of the math award for this year has been chosen." I can tell that most of the kids are tuning out, because a) they're not in the running for it, and b) they don't really care. But I perk up, because a) I *do* care, and b) it's way too early for the math award to be given out. Usually they do it at the end of the year. But maybe something happened and they decided to do it early this year, so all my not-so-great grades aren't going to count, and I'll have won the math scholarship.

I pay attention and sit up in my seat.

But Ms. Kellogg says, "After a careful review, it's been determined that it's now statistically impossible for anyone other than this year's recipient to win the math award. So everyone please congratulate Parvati Carlson for her amazing work this year."

A few people clap, and a guy named Tyler Mansoon yells, "Way to go, Parvati, you work that math, girl!" but other than that, no one seems to care. Except for me. It's weird, because it's not like I really expected to win. In fact, deep down, I kind of knew I didn't have that much of a chance. But now, hearing it being taken away already, I kind of . . . I feel like I let myself down.

"Now, Parvati is very excited about this, and I hope you will all give her the recognition she deserves and use her example and work ethic as something to strive for." I'm not sure, but I think that last part might be just for me. Great. Add Ms. Kellogg to the list of people

I've disappointed, right after my parents, Mackenzie, and my sister.

"Thank you," Parvati says, standing up. Ms. Kellogg looks a little shocked, since it soon becomes apparent that Parvati intends to give some sort of speech, like she thinks she just won a Grammy or an Oscar or something. "I really couldn't have done it without the support of my parents, and Ms. Kellogg here, and my new boyfriend, Josh." She beams at all of us. "When Ms. Kellogg told me I won this morning, I was so thrilled. I'm finally going to be able to afford that new car I wanted, and I hope everyone will keep in touch when I'm at Harvard or Wellesley next year."

She smiles and then sits down daintily in her seat.

So she knew. She knew she had won the whole time she was giving me crap about being in the library with Max. And then Parvati turns around and gives me a big smile.

Okay, maybe I don't feel so bad after all.

♥ ♠ ♣ ♦

When I get to work, Mackenzie is sitting in the employee lounge, eating a salad of olives and goat cheese.

"Hey," I say. I stopped off at Adrienne's office before I came in here, and told her I was supposed to have informed her that Mackenzie wouldn't be at work yesterday. Adrienne was surprisingly cool about it, I think mostly because it was kind of dead in here last night, so it wasn't that big of a deal.

It could also be because Mackenzie's absence

yesterday was the least of Adrienne's worries after I told her I had to quit immediately because of a "family emergency." She was more focused on being pissed about that than about Mackenzie.

"Hi," Mackenzie sniffs. She takes a big bite of salad and shoves it into her mouth. "I would offer you some of my salad, but I know how much you hate goat cheese." She doesn't say it in an "I want to make up with you by offering you some of my salad" kind of way, though. It's more of an "I intentionally ordered my food with goat cheese just because I know you hate it" kind of way.

"That's okay," I say. I sit down next to her. "But, um, listen, I talked to Adrienne, and it's fine, it's cool, she doesn't care that you weren't here."

"Fine," Mackenzie says. She doesn't look up from her magazine.

"That's it?" I ask. "Fine?"

"Yes," she says.

"Okay." I take a deep breath and try to think of a way to tell Mackenzie that I'm not going to be working here anymore.

"You know," Mackenzie says before I can think of anything better than "family emergency." She slams her magazine shut. "You could have at least said you were sorry."

"I did say I was sorry," I reply, shifting slightly in my seat. "I am *so* sorry, really, I am. But Adrienne doesn't care, she's not even mad!"

"You think I care about Adrienne?" Mackenzie asks. She throws her hands up in exasperation and regards me over the table, her blue eyes flashing. "Since when have I ever cared about what *Adrienne* thinks?"

I frown. "I don't get it," I say. "Weren't you mad because I forgot to tell Adrienne you weren't coming to work, therefore putting your job in jeopardy?"

"You think I care about this *job*?" Mackenzie hisses.

"Well, yeah," I say.

"I was *mad*," Mackenzie says, "because we are *supposed* to be friends. And you didn't come through for me, and I got my feelings hurt."

Oh. Suddenly, I feel like a complete and total jerk. And I'm kind of flattered, too. I mean, when I first started working here, I felt like Mackenzie hated me. And now she's more worried about my hurting her feelings than she is about keeping her job.

"I'm so sorry," I say. I take a deep breath. "I've been kind of flaky lately."

"Uh, ya think?" she says. "Is this about that guy you've been seeing? Because honestly, Shannon, you shouldn't be ignoring your girls for some guy." She wrinkles her nose. "And really, I should know, because I totally did the same thing with Lance."

"Look," I say, leaning in close to her, "can you keep a secret?" And then I tell her the whole story.

♥ ♠ ♣ ♦

When I get home, there's music coming from my parents' room, which is weird. My parents don't really *do* music. They don't have iPods, they've never even

232

heard of iTunes, and they have a very limited CD collection and an old boom box that sometimes gets pulled out if they're having a Christmas party or something.

But now some Billy Joel is blasting from their room. Sounds like "Only the Good Die Young." I take it as a good sign, like maybe they've decided that even though I did something bad, they need to let me live my life to the fullest.

"Hey," I say, stepping into their bedroom. "What's going on?" My mom is standing in front of the mirror in a long flowing black dress. She's sliding big silver hoop earrings through her ears. My dad sticks his head out of the closet. He's wearing dress pants and a button-up shirt with a tie.

"Today," my mom announces proudly, "your sister received a scholarship for UMass. She's going to be transferring next year!"

"Wow," I say. "That's awesome." For a second, it's like everything's back to normal, but then I realize that everyone's still mad at me. And that my sister is doing everything right, working hard and getting scholarships, and I'm like some kind of loser who has broken the law and gambled and looked for shortcuts to get ahead.

"I'm ready!" Robyn says, appearing in the doorway. She's wearing a short sparkly silver dress and strappy glittery heels, and her hair is loose and flowing around her shoulders. "Ready to partyyyy!" She does a little twirl around the room. "Oh," she says, stopping short when she sees me. "Shannon, what are you doing here?"

"I had to quit my job, remember?" I say. "So I did and then I came home. Why is everyone so dressed up?"

"We're going out to celebrate," my mom says. "I made reservations at Anthony Jacks. I only made them for three, but I can call back and change it if you'd like to join us." I see my mom and dad look at each other, and all of a sudden it's awkward.

"Uh, no," I say. "That's okay. I actually have a ton of homework to do." The truth is as much as I'd like to celebrate my sister's accomplishment, I just don't think I could stand to sit there and pretend that everything's okay. And I'm pretty sure it's not my imagination that my family looks relieved.

14

The next morning, I throw on a T-shirt and some track pants and head out to meet Cole before school. He called last night as I was getting ready for bed and asked me where I was. I told him that I'd quit my job, and that my parents had been freaking out, and that I had to lie low for the next few nights. He didn't seem that upset or suspicious, but I asked him to meet me before school, because I figure I should see him in person so that I can convince him I'm really up for fixing the tournament.

"Rough night, Shannon Card?" he asks when he sees me. We're in the parking lot of Starbucks, and he's leaning against the back of his Escalade. Cole, who I know has almost definitely been up all night, looks fresh as a daisy. He's wearing a gray T-shirt, a pair of jeans, and his leather jacket. His face is stubbly, and even though I know it's just because he hasn't gotten around to shaving, it looks intentional, like he's cultivating that sexily scruffy look. And he does look sexily scruffy, with his hair all wild and hanging in his face.

"Not really," I say. "But, listen, I wanted to tell you again in person that I'm in. With the plan, I mean. One hundred percent."

He grins. "I knew you'd come around," he says. He takes a sip of his coffee. Cole got here before me and didn't even wait to get a drink or ask me if I wanted one. I mean, honestly. He really needs better manners. Although I suppose his manners should be the least of my worries. I should be more concerned about his penchant for illegal activities.

"You did?"

"Yeah," he says. "You're a smart girl, Shannon, and I think you have a lot of potential."

I resist the urge to roll my eyes.

"So listen," he says, checking his watch, "I have to get going, but I'll see you later? Do you want to play tonight?"

"I'm not sure," I say, annoyed that he's trying to ditch me already. Probably he's tired and needs to get back to his hotel room. Seriously, what a jerk. "I could probably sneak out if I really wanted to, but . . ." I trail off, hoping he doesn't call my bluff. Ever since I challenged him that night at Logan's, something has shifted between us, and I don't think he wants to hang out with me any more than I want to hang out with him. But he can't let me know that, because I'm another person he's going to have working for him during the tournament, and he doesn't want to lose me.

"That's okay," he says. "I think we should probably take a break until the tournament in a couple weeks," he says. He reaches out and brushes a piece of my hair out of my face. "Just chill out a little bit."

"Good idea," I say.

"I should probably hold off on having too many late nights," he says. "I have to focus on school. But I'll call you and let you know what's going on." And then he winks at me.

It's so totally obvious that he's blowing me off. And it's even more obvious that he thinks I'm buying all his bullshit. But I know I have to play it cool, so I just smile and pretend I believe him.

♥　♠　♣　♦

By the time I get to school, I. Am. So. Mad. Max is pulling his car into the parking lot at the same time I am, so I take the spot next to his, then get out of my car and climb into the passenger seat of his.

"So get this," I say, slamming the door shut with all my might.

"Whoa," Max says. "Chill, this car isn't getting any younger." But he's laughing.

"Sorry," I say sheepishly. "I'm just SO MAD. I just came from seeing Cole and he told me—" I look at Max. "Are you ready for this?"

"Yes," he says, nodding seriously. "I'm ready for this."

"He told me that he has to 'hold off on having too many late nights.' " I use air quotes to show just how completely ridiculous I think that is.

"Wow," Max says. "Way to blow you off."

"I know!" I say. "And after I totally got left out of our family dinner last night for my sister's big celebration!"

"What do you mean?" he asks. So I fill him in on how everyone went out without me. How I stayed in my room, trying to fall asleep until I heard them come home, laughing and talking about the food and the fun. How then they pulled ice cream out of the freezer even though apparently they'd already had dessert at the restaurant. And suddenly, my eyes are filling with tears, and I lean my head back against the headrest in Max's car.

"Hey, hey," Max says. "It's going to be okay." He puts his arm around me and he pulls me in close to him, and it's nice and he smells like soap and apple shampoo.

"I'm sorry," I say, pulling away. "All I'm doing lately is crying all over you."

I'm afraid to look up at him, because then our lips will be very close, and I'm not sure if I trust myself.

"It's okay," he says. "I kind of like it."

My phone beeps then. A text from Cole. "Maybe we should hang out tonight after all."

"Oh. My. God," I say, showing Max. "Total booty call!"

"Total," Max says.

"He," I say, my eyes narrowing, "is so going down."

♥ ♠ ♣ ♦

Over the next two weeks, the following things happen:

1. I become a very good actress. This is because I'm now playing two challenging roles: a) that of the girlfriend who is too stupid to realize that her boyfriend is blowing her off and possibly hooking up with Michelle, and b) that of a girl who is going along with Aces Up's plan to fix the poker tournament, even though she is totally opposed to it.

2. I get together for two meetings with Aces Up, where we learn the signals we're going to be using for the tournament. Nothing big, basically just things like little stretches and pokes, to let people know when to bet or to fold or whatever. I looked it up online, and what they're doing is called collusion, and it's pretty serious.

3. Other than sneaking out for these meetings with Aces, I am being a model daughter and student. I go home, do my homework, and then spend the rest of my time in bed, talking on the phone to Max or listening to music. Of course my parents still have no idea about the tournament, but honestly, I can't tell them. They wouldn't let me do it, they'd make me quit, they'd make me turn Aces Up in, and I could definitely get in trouble then. Bye-bye Wellesley. I'm probably not going to have the money to go to Wellesley now anyway, but I'd rather have to delay my admission because of financial reasons than because it was revoked. Plus I really don't think I can stand disappointing my parents even more than they already are.

4. Max and I don't kiss again. And even though it's been a little bit flirty at times, I can't help thinking maybe he really does only like me as a friend. And it's fine, because I'm glad to have him back, in whatever way I can.

The night before the National Championship of Poker, I tiptoe to the door of Robyn's room and knock on it softly. I can hear her typing on the computer, so I assume she's working on a paper or maybe IM'ing with Leonardo.

"Come in," she says, and I open the door and scoot into her room, shutting it behind me.

"Hi," I say.

"Oh," she says. "Hey." She seems surprised that it's me, and I don't blame her. We haven't really talked since she told my parents what happened. Which is horrible, when you think about it. I mean, she's my best friend. At least, I hope she still is.

"Um, I just wanted to say hi," I say lamely. "And give you back this." I hold out a T-shirt I borrowed from her a few weeks ago and never got around to giving back.

Robyn looks back and forth from me to the shirt.

"Are you serious?" she asks. She reaches out and touches the fabric.

"Um, yeah," I say. "I know I've had it for a while, but it was in the bottom of my laundry bag and I didn't realize it until just now."

And then Robyn bursts into tears, right there in front of her computer.

"Hey, hey, hey," I say. "Why are you crying?" Is my sister that worked up over a T-shirt? Wow. I really should have returned it a lot sooner. I had no idea clothes made her so emotional.

"Because," she says, sniffling. "Because I totally told on you, I totally broke our trust of sisterhood, and it was only because I was worried about you, but I don't know why I even did it . . . *and I just feel horrible and now we hate each other!*"

241

"You hate me?" I ask.

"No-ooo," she wails. "But you hate me, so I was just pretending I was ignoring you so that I wouldn't have to deal with the fact that *you* were ignoring *me*."

"So you were pretending that the ignoring was your idea?"

"Yes," she says. She plucks a tissue off the box on her desk and blows her nose. Robyn always has tissues around, because when you're dating Leonardo, you never know when you're going to be having a good cry.

"Well, it worked," I say. "I really did think you were ignoring me. But I'm really, really glad that you weren't."

She smiles at me through her tears. "Shannon, what the hell is going on? I mean, why didn't you talk to me, why didn't you . . ."

So I take a deep breath. And then I tell her everything, just like I told Max, and just like I told Mackenzie. About Cole. About the poker. About Cole's plan, and about my plan. And about Max, and Wellesley.

"Wow," she says when I'm done. "Just wow."

"I know, right?" I say. "I mean, nothing like this *ever* happens to me, you know?"

"Um, nothing like this ever happens to anyone," she says. "So now you have to go along with their plan?"

"Yeah," I say. "Just for this one tournament, and then I'm done, I swear."

Robyn hesitates for a second, like she wants to say something else, and for a horrible moment I'm afraid she's going to insist we tell my parents. But finally she just nods.

"And, Robyn?" I say. "You did the right thing, telling Mom and Dad. I love you." And then I give her a hug.

♥ ♠ ♣ ♦

The morning of the tournament dawns bright and clear, and I take that as a good sign. I'm always better when the sun's out. I dress in my jeans and light blue zip-up hoodie. Screw Cole and his "you have to look sexy to play sexy" or whatever his stupid theory is. I say you have to dress comfortably to play well. Or at least to, you know, trick your underground poker society into thinking you're a cheater.

When I get outside to my driveway, there's a car parked in it along with mine. It's not Robyn's. Or Leonardo's. Or Mackenzie's. Or my parents'. It's a car I don't recognize. Ohmigod. What if Cole sent someone here to escort me to the tournament? What if he sent someone here to threaten me? Or worse, what if he found out my plan, and he sent someone here to make sure I cooperate? I'm about two seconds away from screaming when Max pokes his head out of the driver's side window.

"Hey," he says. "I thought we could go together."

♥ ♠ ♣ ♦

He brought me a coffee! A Starbucks coffee with sugar-free Cinnamon Dolce syrup, which is my absolute favorite coffee ever. And he remembered! He was paying attention and listening, and he brought me a coffee, and that is so super-sweet. And he even had to borrow his mom's car, since his is in the shop, getting new tires. He totally went out of his way for me.

I know that doesn't necessarily *mean* anything. I get Robyn coffees all the time. I'm sure he was just being nice. I know from reading *He's Just Not That Into You* that if a guy isn't kissing you, he's, you know, just not that into you.

Still.

I covertly text Mackenzie on the way to the tournament: "Max brought me coffee this morning and totally remembered what I liked, what do you think about that?"

The reply comes immediately: "He totally wants you!!!!!"

My face turns red, and I hope Max doesn't notice. We're riding over together. He insisted. He said that I needed to decompress on the car ride and clear my head.

What he doesn't know is that I'm way more nervous riding over with him, because now all I can think about is that he brought me coffee, and that Mackenzie says he wants me. Not that I think she means he wants to have sex with me, but more that she means he's interested in me. Doesn't she? Oh, God. Maybe she *does* mean that he just wants to have sex. That wouldn't be so great. I've had enough of guys who just wanted to have sex with me. Not that Cole just wanted me for sex, but he definitely just wanted to hook up.

This is all very confusing. I'm contemplating sending Mackenzie a follow-up text for clarification, but we're pulling into the garage of the casino, so I make a mental note to ask her later.

"You ready?" Max asks.

"Ready!" I say. But I'm really nervous. The tournament is going to be starting in an hour. One. Hour. What if it doesn't work? What if they figure out what I'm doing? What if they turn me in for being underage? What if they kill me? What if they—

"You can do this," Max says. He puts his hand on my shoulder and rubs it softly.

"Right," I say, my voice strangled.

"Think about it," he says. "In a few hours, this whole thing will be over."

"Max—" I say, then swallow. But Max is out of the car and over on my side now, opening the door for me. I get out, and I don't know if it's all the caffeine or what, but I'm a little wobbly.

"Hellooooo! Wait for me, wait for me!" Robyn's voice screeches across the parking garage, followed by Robyn herself. She's wearing a long black dress and high heels, which are making clicking noises as she runs.

"Why didn't you tell me you were leaving?" she says, out of breath from running. "I heard the car starting up, and I followed you all the way here." She puts a pout on her face. "I had to do my makeup in the car!"

"I didn't know you wanted to come," I say. My parents left early this morning to visit my Grandma Card, and they put Robyn in charge of me. They didn't *say* that exactly, but it's totally what they meant. They said I could leave the house as long as Robyn was with me, so I figured Robyn would cover for me and tell them we were together during the day, but I had no idea she'd actually come to the tournament with me.

"Of course I wanted to come," she says. "Did you think I wouldn't be here?" She squeezes my arm, and I grab her in a hug.

"Hey," Max says to Robyn as we walk toward the elevators.

"Hey, Max," Robyn says. "Nice to see you."

"You too," Max says. And then, when he's not looking, she elbows me in the side. I grin. Robyn and I are definitely back to normal.

When we get inside to the tournament room, Robyn and Max hightail it to the refreshments cart, and I find Cole, who's leaning against the wall, looking bored. The tournament is going to start in half an hour.

"Hey," I say, pushing him in the shoulder.

"Hey, Shannon Card," he says lazily. Hmmm. His eyes look a little bit weird. He could definitely be hung over. Not the best way to start the tournament, but whatever. Maybe he's like one of those artists who need to be drunk to do their best work. "I like what you're wearing," he says sarcastically.

"Thanks," I say, ignoring the sarcasm. I figure the stupider I can convince him I am, the better. Not that it matters. It's all going to be over soon enough, anyway. I take a deep breath and try to calm my beating heart.

"You excited?" he asks.

"Totally." And then I kiss him on the cheek, turn around, and head to my seat.

The tournament actually starts out kind of boring. For the first couple of hours, I don't get very many good cards, there are tons of people still in, and I don't end up at a table with any of the other Aces Up members. I'm doing okay on my chip count, winning a few little pots here and there, but honestly, I'm not really seeing that much action. Which is fine. The fewer chips I accumulate, the better. In fact, if I didn't think it would look too obvious, I would get rid of all my chips immediately.

We have a few breaks, when I eat sandwiches and grab coffee and go to the bathroom. I need to stay focused, so I don't talk to Robyn and Max, who are sitting against the wall together. I just hope my sister isn't saying anything embarrassing (like "What are your intentions toward my sister?" and "How do you feel about marriage?"), but I can't really worry about that now. I have to focus on getting through this.

Finally, around two o'clock, they combine the

tables again, and I end up at a table with Michelle. Basically, if we're in a hand together, one of us should fold, and if we're not, we should signal to each other what to do. For the first few hands, neither one of us sees any action. And then, finally, I get dealt queen, king.

I bet into the pot, and the flop comes queen, nine, five.

Michelle signals at me not to bet. That must mean she has something and wants me to stay out of the pot, so that we're not competing with each other and scaring people off. But normally, I would bet here, and her signal is so clear that I think if anyone was to watch the tapes later, they would know. So I bet. I watch as Michelle frowns and then rolls her eyes and looks at me with disgust. I can tell by the expression on her face that she thinks I forgot the signals. I guess that's one good thing about her hating me—she already thinks I'm dumb, so she won't be too suspicious.

Sure enough, when we get up for the next break, she gives me a poke in the side on her way to the bathroom. "You're misreading the signals," she says, and gives me a look like she thinks I'm stupid. "I told you to fold."

"Oh," I say, blinking really fast. "Sorry, I thought you said to bet. I thought you were supposed to be taking my chips." I shrug, and she rolls her eyes at me again and then takes off. I turn on my heel and go to find Max and Robyn.

♥ ♠ ♣ ♦

"Okay," Robyn says, "just breathe. Honestly, it's going to be fine."

"No, it's not," I say. We're in the back hallway, outside the ballroom where the tournament's being held. I'm sitting on one of the folding chairs against the wall, and Robyn is standing next to me. She gathers my hair into a ponytail and starts fanning the back of my neck with her hand. Like I said, up until this point, I've kind of been avoiding Max and Robyn, since a) I need to keep my concentration, and b) I don't want Cole to think anything's up when he sees that I've brought friends with me. But this was just too much to handle on my own.

"They're going to know." I lean forward in my chair and try not to faint.

"What do you mean?" Max asks, frowning.

"I *mean*," I say, "that they're going to realize that I'm pretending to go along with it, but that I'm really not."

"No, I know that's what you meant," Max says. He sits down in the chair next to me and takes my hand, rubbing my forearm. "I just mean what specifically makes you think they're going to realize what you're doing?"

"They're assholes," I say, "but unfortunately, they're not stupid. And eventually, I'm not going to be able to pretend anymore." I tell him what just happened with Michelle.

Max studies me for a long moment, and then he

nods. "Did she believe you when you said you misread the signal?"

"I think so," I say. "But she might not for long."

"I'm late!" someone yells, tearing through the crowd. I look up to see Mackenzie, dressed in her work uniform. "I'm supposed to be working this tournament, and I'm late!" Her face is all flushed, and her high heels are slipping and sliding into the plush carpet. "I had a late night," she explains, and then gives me a wink. I can only imagine what that means.

"Hi," she says, putting her hand out to Max. "How are you doing, Max?"

"I'm good," he says.

Then Mackenzie turns to Robyn. "And you," she says, narrowing her eyes, "must be the sister."

"Yeah," Robyn says. "How did you know?"

"Just had a feeling," Mackenzie says. She and Robyn size each other up for a second, and I can tell what each of them is thinking. Robyn's wondering how Mackenzie could have worked with me all this time and let me fall into such a dangerous situation, and Mackenzie's wondering why Robyn would have made such a big deal over me doing something as silly as gambling.

But I don't have time to get caught up in any drama.

"Guys," I hiss. "What do I do?"

"Relax," Max says, reaching over and squeezing my hand. "You're going to be fine." And then . . . He. Doesn't. Take. His. Hand. Back. Max Heller is holding my hand. In front of everyone here. In front of hundreds of people, he is holding my hand like it's not a big deal. And then there's a tap on my shoulder.

I turn around. Cole.

"Oh, hello!" Mackenzie says brightly. I drop Max's hand like it's poisonous or something.

"I need to talk to you," Cole says, ignoring her.

"Sure," I say confidently. I follow him to the side of the casino.

"What the hell is going on?" Wow. He's really angry. I've never seen him this angry.

"Wow," I say. "I've never seen you this angry."

"Yeah, well, maybe that's because you've never done anything this stupid." And then I see something shift in his face. It's like he goes from what he's really feeling (anger and like maybe he wants to wring my neck) to some kind of mode in which he realizes that's *so* not the way to get what he wants from me. "Sorry," he says, reaching out and running his hand up my arm. I shiver. And not in a good way. Then his face changes again. "Look," he says, "what are you doing?"

I take a deep breath and summon up my resolve. "Playing poker," I say.

"Michelle said you weren't listening to her signals," he says. He's smiling, but his eyes are cold.

"You can't listen to the signals," I say. "They're nonauditory." Wow. I didn't even know I knew that word. Nonauditory. Sounds like something a very smart person would say, one who's a force to be reck-oned with.

"You know what I mean," he says. He's still moving his hand up and down my arm, so I lean into him.

"Not really," I say. "And I just got confused." I give him a pleading look. "There were so many things to remember, and I didn't even get to go to any of the last few meetings." I pout my lips out and try to seem like I've missed him these past few weeks.

For a second, he looks at me skeptically, and I'm positive he's going to tell me he knows I'm not that stu-pid. But then his face softens. "Ooh . . . so that's what this is about." He breaks into that cocky grin of his and leans back against the wall.

I frown. "That's what *what* is about?"

"You're jealous."

"Jealous? Of what?"

"Of Michelle," Cole says. "Look, there's nothing going on between me and her."

Ohmigod. I can't believe it! He thinks I wasn't paying attention to Michelle's signals because I'm trying to get back at her for flirting or something equally ridiculous. I'm so shocked that for a second, I can't talk, and Cole takes my "you're so crazy I don't even know how to respond" silence as my agree-ing with his stupid theory. "Did Logan tell you we hooked up?"

"Did Logan tell me who hooked up?" This is all getting way too confusing.

"Me and Michelle," Cole says. "We did hook up, but it was, like, forever ago."

Ohmigod. Not that it's a big surprise. I mean, from the beginning, it was totally obvious that the two of them had some sort of history. And actually, they probably have some sort of present, as well.

My blood starts to boil and I want to do something bad. Like maybe slap him or something. Or throw a drink in his face, like they're always doing in movies. But all I do is say, "Well, it would have been nice if you'd told me you guys had hooked up. I didn't want to have to hear it from Logan."

"Don't be mad, Shannon Card." He flashes me his "you know you love me" smile, and this time, it doesn't charm me. But I pretend it does.

"I'm not mad," I say, smiling. "I'm not mad at all."

"Good," he says, visibly relaxing. "So then we're back on the same page."

"Yes," I say. "Totally. I'm really sorry that I let my personal problem with Michelle interfere with my playing." He holds out his arms and I give him a hug, and then we head back to the tables.

♥ ♠ ♣ ♦

"He thinks he can play you?" Mackenzie asks. "He thinks he can MESS WITH THIS?"

Mackenzie, Robyn, and I are in the bathroom during the next break of the tournament, and I have just relayed what went down. Max is waiting outside, because, hello, he can't come in the girls' bathroom and I really

254

had to pee. Mackenzie keeps bringing me extra Diet Cokes and refusing to take tips from me. ("But I will not bring *that girl* any drinks, and I won't bring Cole any drinks, either, that nasty jerk.")

"What do you mean?" I ask, frowning.

"I mean," she says, "that he thinks he can just mess with you like that, that he thinks he can just say, 'Oh, you're jealous about some skank, and don't worry, nothing is going on between us.' "

"Oh," I say. "Then yeah. He does. Think he can mess with this, I mean." By "this," I'm assuming she means me. Or us. Which is kind of nice. Although I don't really know why she seems so surprised, since a guy who is trying to fix a huge poker tournament is probably not too concerned about telling a little lie about who he's hooking up with.

"Well, he's in for a rude awakening," Robyn says. She pats my back. But she doesn't seem so sure. Mackenzie, however, is totally fired up, and she nods, then reaches over and gives Robyn a high five. After a rough start, apparently Robyn and Mackenzie have bonded over girl power and, I'd like to think, their love for me.

"Just keep doing what you're doing," Robyn says, rubbing my back. "You're doing great."

"That's because I haven't actually had to do anything yet," I say. Which is true. There has been a lot of waiting. And I haven't been at Cole's table yet, but that's going to change soon, since the number of tables is getting smaller as people are getting knocked out.

"Hey, guys," Max yells from outside. "They're starting up in two more minutes."

"Great," I say. "Just great." I wash my hands quickly at the sink. "Fill him in for me, will ya?"

"Of course," Robyn says.

♥ ♠ ♣ ♦

It's forty-five minutes later when everything really starts to hit the fan. There are only fifteen people left in the tournament, and finally, I get put at a table with Cole. Michelle has gotten eliminated from the tournament, and I'm assuming she's dumped her chips to Cole, along with a few other people, since he is by far the chip leader. Logan is still in the tournament, and there's one other college kid who's using the signs we all came up with. I'm assuming he's a part of all this but was someone we weren't allowed contact with, just in case anyone got caught.

The first hand at my new table, I get dealt an okay starter hand—ace, jack—and the flop comes jack, eight, eight. Cole bets, and everyone except him, me, and one other person folds. Based on what we talked about, this means that now I should bet, and then Cole will check-raise me, and I'll call. The point is to make it seem like we both have huge hands so that the other guy will get scared away, and in the end, Cole will end up with chips from both of us. But this isn't what I do. Instead, after the turn, I check.

The guy at the end of the table puts in a huge bet. Cole hesitates. Finally, he calls. I fold, and when the river comes, Cole's flush loses to the other guy's full house.

The dealer pushes the huge mound of chips down to the end of the table, and I give Cole a "what are you doing?" look. Like maybe it's his fault and he's the one who didn't play it right, not me. But this time I can tell he's totally not buying it.

♥ ♠ ♣ ♦

At the next break, I don't even have a chance to get to Max and Robyn before Cole grabs my arm and pulls me outside the room.

"What the fuck are you doing?" he says.

"What do you mean?" I ask. I try to play dumb again and thank God that there are cameras throughout the whole casino. My heart is pounding really fast, and I'm afraid. Out of the corner of my eye, I see Max rise from his chair on the other side of the room and cross it in long strides. I try to telegraph to him to just chill, that I can handle it. But Max doesn't listen. Um, either that or he doesn't really get what I'm trying to say.

"Just what I said," Cole says angrily. "You're doing it on purpose."

"No," I say. "I just got confused. I think the signals are—"

"That's ridiculous," he says. "You didn't get confused, you're being stupid, and doing it on purpose, and I want you to tell me WHAT. THE. HELL. IS. GOING. ON."

"Hey," Max says from behind us, grabbing Cole by the sleeve of his leather jacket and spinning him around. "Don't talk to her like that."

"Oh, and who are you?" Cole asks. "The new guy? How cute. Don't waste your time, if you know what I mean." I gasp. He was the one who didn't ever try to go past third base! Mackenzie even said she thought he was gay! Max gasps, too, and then he grabs Cole by the collar.

"I said," Max repeats, "don't talk to her like that."

"I'll talk to her," Cole says, "however I feel like talking to her." His dark eyes are flashing now.

"No," Max says. "You won't." They're staring each other down, and for a second, I think Max is going to punch Cole. But then a casino security guard comes over and says, "Hey! Is there a problem here?"

Neither one of them moves and it's super-scary, because I think maybe it *is* going to be a big problem here, but finally Cole relaxes and turns to the guard. "No," he says. "No problem here." He turns away from Max until Max lets him go. The security guard gives them one more look and then leaves. Cole puts his cocky grin back on, but I can tell he's rattled, and I saw the look of panic that crossed his face. Wow. Cole is afraid of getting caught. The whole time, I totally thought he was this scary guy, with the mob behind him or something. But he's actually kind of . . . lame.

Then Cole does exactly what I was afraid he might do.

He looks at Max and then at me.

And he says, "Go ahead and try to win. It doesn't matter anyway, because I'll just tell them you're underage."

"Yeah," I say. "And if you tell them I'm underage, I'll tell them what you're doing."

For a second, he seems unsure, and I think I just might have scared him into letting me go. But then his grin comes back, and he looks me right in the eye and says, "You mean what *we're* doing." And he pushes past us, back into the tournament room.

"Shannon," Max says, "are you okay?"

"Yeah," I say. "I'm fine." But my knees feel weak and wobbly, and all I want to do is go home. Seriously. Going back into that room suddenly seems like an insurmountable task. Because the thing is, Cole's right.

We are doing this. I know what they're doing, and I'm pretending to go along with it to save my own ass, while not really doing it. But it doesn't matter that I haven't technically been cheating. I know the plan. I'm supposed to be *part* of the plan. And if I turned them all in, I would be in trouble, too. There are hours and hours of Cole and me together on casino security tapes, not just from today, but from the past several weeks. It would be my word against theirs. I was naïve about the whole thing. I thought I could get off scot-free, but honestly, it just isn't going to work out like that.

"Shannon—"

I don't get to hear what Max is going to tell me, because the tournament is starting back up, and I have to take my place at the table. And Cole's there, and he's looking at me all smarmy-like, as if he thinks he's going to be able to get one over on me. In that second, I really do kind of hate him. I take a deep breath and try to calm my thoughts. And then it becomes clear what I have to do.

Turn myself in, so that I can turn *them* in.

Otherwise I'm going to have to go along with their plan, and I still might get caught. If I don't, who knows what they'll do to me? I'll have taken ten thousand dollars from them, and I don't know that they're going to take that lightly.

So that's it. It's over. Everything. Wellesley will be gone. My parents will be pissed all over again. And who knows what other horrible things might happen? It's kind of a relief, actually, to know that this whole thing is going to be done.

But first I'm going to beat these jerks. I slide into my seat and get ready to play.

♥ ♠ ♣ ♦

After that, I'm kind of on autopilot. I play and run the percentages in my head and make the moves I'm supposed to. And I start to knock out the players of Aces Up one by one. Actually, that's not quite true. I get most of Logan's chips in a big hand he probably shouldn't have played and then Joe dumps the rest of his chips to Cole.

We play for hours. It's almost two in the morning, and I'm starting to think that this is never going to end. Robyn, Max, and Mackenzie have all stayed with me the whole time. Robyn calls my parents and tells them we're spending the night at her friend Nicole's house. Mackenzie keeps bringing me drinks, and Max keeps coming over to my table and rubbing my back.(!!!)

Finally, it's down to just four people. Me, Cole, and two other guys who are definitely not in Aces Up. They're older, and I haven't caught them using any of the signals we agreed on.

I am dealt a three and a seven, but I'm in the big blind, and no one raises, so I'm allowed to look at the flop for free.

The flop comes three, jack, jack, giving me two pair. Cole checks, I bet, and the other two guys fold. Cole looks me right in the eye as he calls. Geez. What a jerk. Seriously, he's about one step away from, like, threatening me or hissing at me or something. Weird.

The next card, the turn, is a king. Cole bets out, and I have to think about it. The smart move might be to fold. I have two pair, but there's definitely a chance that Cole has a jack in his hand, giving him three of a kind, or he could have king, jack, which would give him a full house. To make matters even worse, there are three hearts on the board, which means that Cole could have a flush. And even if he has only one heart in his hand, there's a chance another heart could come on the river, allowing him to make his flush.

All around us, the casino is quiet as I run the options in my head. There are so many different possibilities and variables in this particular hand that it's making it hard.

I take a deep breath and get ready to fold. I think it makes the most sense to get out of the hand; I'll just have to hope there will be other places, better places, times when I know I will have a better chance of knocking Cole out. I just have to be patient for a little longer. I take another deep breath and get ready to muck my hand. But then I catch Max's eye across the casino, and I realize that sometimes everything doesn't have to make sense. I look at Cole then, really study his face, and try to see if I can pick anything up.

Something tells me that he doesn't have a hand. So I call his bet. The last card comes the five of spades, which means that if Cole has a king, a jack, or a five, I'm definitely screwed.

He bets, a smaller bet to try to lure me in. Or at least, that's what he wants me to think. But really he's bluffing. So I raise him.

"I'm all in," Cole says, looking right at me. And for a second, I falter. What if he really does have a hand? But then he says, "What are you gonna do, Shannon Card?" and when I hear the cocky tone in his voice, it becomes clear. Cole's been all talk this whole time. About everything. So why would anything change now?

"I call," I say. And before I can stop myself, I push all my chips into the middle of the table.

♥ ♠ ♣ ♦

It totally feels like one of those movies, where everyone is waiting for the big reveal and things are moving in slow motion. I turn my cards over, showing Cole that I have two pair.

Cole turns his over. The ace of diamonds and the queen of clubs. Cole has nothing. Everything stops for a second, and Cole is just sitting there, looking down at the table like he can't believe it.

Max and Mackenzie and Robyn come over and they're all screaming and jumping around, and Robyn's hugging me and it's like I'm a rock star or something. And when I turn around, Cole is gone.

And then Max is holding me close, and for a second, I can kind of forget that none of this matters because I am about to be in deep, deep trouble. But then the reality of the situation hits again. When Max whispers, "Do you want me to go with you?" into my ear, I shake my head. I pull away and look at him. "How did you know?" I ask.

He shrugs. "I just did." And then he smiles, and I smile back.

♥ ♠ ♣ ♦

I purposely lose on the next few hands. I try to distribute my chips evenly to the two guys who are left, and for the most part, it works. Of course, they're totally confused by what's going on, and the dealer looks like maybe she thinks I'm on crack or something.

Once I'm eliminated, I calmly get up from my chair

and walk toward the check-in table. And then I say to the pit boss, "Excuse me, sir? I'd like to turn myself in."

♥ ♠ ♣ ♦

They bring me to a room in the back and make me wait while they call in Adrienne, the head pit boss, and the head of operations. They take my cell phone, I guess so I can't call anyone and try to get my story straight. They give me a small bottle of water, which I drain in about one minute, and then I just sit in the room, in a very uncomfortable chair, trying to keep my heart from beating out of my chest.

I am so scared. I have no idea what they're going to do to me. I'm definitely going to be in trouble with my family, and at this point, Wellesley doesn't even matter, because I'm sure they don't take felons.

Finally, after what seems like forever but is probably only about fifteen minutes, the door to the room bursts open, and two scary-looking men followed by Adrienne come into the room.

"Shannon Card?" the scariest-looking guy asks.

"Yes," I say, standing up and holding my hand out. Why oh why am I wearing a sweatshirt and jeans? Definitely not proper attire when you're trying to convince someone not to arrest you. He shakes it, and even his hand feels scary.

"Rich Benton," he says. "Head of casino operations."

"Shannon Card," I say. I'm about to add "cocktail

waitress" but then decide against it, since I don't work there anymore.

"Sit," Mr. Benton says, and I sit. So does Adrienne, but as she sits down, she looks at me with a death glare.

"This is Clyde Marris," Mr. Benton says, "the pit boss you just spoke with."

I give him a half smile, but Clyde doesn't smile back.

"Is it true what you just told him?" Mr. Benton asks. "That you entered the National Championship of Poker and that you had been participating in collusion and other activities that are deemed illegal?"

"Yes," I whisper. "But I wasn't really . . . I mean, I didn't technically *do* anything. But I was part of the plan, yes."

"And you do understand, Shannon, that what you did was illegal, and that if we so choose, we could prosecute you to the full extent of the law?"

"Yes," I whisper again. Visions of myself in a prison-issued orange jumpsuit dance through my head. Actually, I'll probably end up in juvenile hall. Unless they decide to try me as an adult. I start to feel a little nauseous and I try to take a sip out of my water bottle before I realize there's no water left.

"Good," Mr. Benton says. "Now we also need to discuss the issue of your being underage. One of the other tournament participants, a man named Cole Porter, claims you're only seventeen." So he did turn me in! He got pissed that I beat him, and so he

265

turned me in, figuring I would never turn *them* in, because I'd get in trouble, too. Not that I'm surprised. But still.

"Yes," I say. "That's true, too."

He starts to talk again, but my head is spinning so much that I don't know exactly what he's saying, but I'm sure there are lots of issues to discuss, and the next thing I know, the whole room is getting a little bit wobbly. "I think," I say slowly, "that I need some more water."

I must look like I'm about to keel over, because Adrienne's eyes get all wide and she says, "Get her some water, she needs some water!" and then Clyde rushes out and comes back a minute later with a bottle of water, and I take a few sips and start to feel better.

"Now," Mr. Benton says. "Are you okay?"

"Yes," I say. "I'm feeling better."

"We might," he says, "be willing to overlook your minor status and strike some kind of deal. If you tell us more about the cheating that's been going on here at the Collosio."

"The cheating?"

"Yes," Mr. Benton says. He leans over his desk. "We don't like cheaters here."

"Of course not," I say. "Who likes cheaters?"

"So are you willing to do it?" he asks.

I look at him. "You're telling me that if I turn in the people who have been cheating, and let you know how they've been cheating and what their plan was, we could possibly strike some sort of a deal?"

"Yes," Mr. Benton says. He leans back in his chair, folds his hands in front of him, and waits for me to talk.

"Um, can I get that in writing?" I ask.

♥ ♠ ♣ ♦

On my way out of the office, I see one of the security guards hustling Cole in. Cole gives me a really dirty look as I pass, but I just keep walking. I can't believe I was hooking up with that guy every single night. Eww.

When I get into the lobby near the tournament area, Robyn, Mackenzie, and Max are all waiting for me.

"Oh my God," Mackenzie yells, and runs over to me. She grabs me in a huge hug, almost knocking me backward. "Max told us what happened. We were so worried!"

"I know," I say. Suddenly, I'm exhausted. I don't know if it's from lack of sleep, or stress, or both, but all I want to do is curl up and close my eyes.

"So what was going on?" Robyn asks. "We saw Cole getting arrested by the police!"

"That wasn't the police," I say. "That was casino security, and they were bringing him in for questioning."

Robyn's eyes get wide. "Questioning?"

"Yes," I say. "But he's in a lot of trouble, and he's probably going to be arrested."

"Oh my God!" Mackenzie screams.

"Are *you* in a lot of trouble?" Robyn asks, biting her lip.

"Sort of," I say. "I mean, they said they can probably cut me some kind of deal if I tell them everything I know. But I'm going to need a lawyer. And I'm definitely going to need to tell Mom and Dad."

Robyn nods. "I'll do it with you," she says.

"Thanks," I say. "But I really think I need to do this on my own."

"I can't believe you were hooking up with that guy," Mackenzie says. "He is a complete and total rat bastard."

"Rat bastard?" And I can't help it. I burst out laughing.

So does everyone else.

♥ ♠ ♣ ♦

Robyn takes her car home, and then Mackenzie takes *her* car home after I promise to call her later and tell her how everything turns out with my parents.

So then it's just me and Max, and I'm not ready to go home yet, because it's too . . . I don't know. I feel like I need a little bit of time before I go home to face my parents and deal with everything that goes along with that. It's four in the morning, and I know that when Robyn gets home without me they are going to be flipping out. So Max takes me to a twenty-four-hour Wendy's and we order chocolate Frosties and French fries and sit in the parking lot, eating.

"Crazy day, huh?" he says.

"Yeah," I say. I take a fry and slide it into my mouth. I'm surprised I can eat, but somehow even though during the tournament I was too anxious to be hungry, now I'm suddenly starving and resisting the urge to just shove fries into my mouth.

"You did really great," he says. He reaches over, takes my hand, and draws little circles on it with his thumb.

"I did?" I say.

"Yeah."

"But I don't have money for Wellesley," I say. "And I don't have a job."

"You'll figure it out," he says simply.

"How do you know?"

He looks right at me and says, "Because I do."

"I don't know," I say. "I'm . . ." I turn and stare out the car window, thinking about everything that's gone down the past couple of months. How could I have been so stupid? How could I have lost myself so much that I got caught up in such bad things? What are my parents going to think when I tell them that I've lied to them again? Am I really that bad a judge of character? And if so, how *can* I know that everything's going to be all right?

"Hey," Max says, and he reaches out and pulls my chin toward him. As if he's reading my mind, he says, "Let me prove it to you." And then he kisses me, and he tastes like chocolate and French fries and everything good, and just for one second, he's right. I forget about everything else and pretend it's all fine.

269

FROM THE TRANSFER APPLICATION TO WELLESLEY UNIVERSITY, PAGE 4:

Please explain any special circumstances that may help us in reaching a transfer decision. Please include any information you think is applicable to the admissions process.

Last year, my early admission status to Wellesley was revoked when I was put on probation due to illegally gambling at the Collosio Casino in Connecticut. Additionally, my senior-year grades dropped substantially, and these two things made me an unsuitable candidate for Wellesley.

I made some horrible choices during that time and alienated a lot of people close to me. However, I am happy to say that my relationships with my family and friends are now the best they've ever been. My parents, while always supportive, are impressed with the way I've turned things around and the positive attitude I've displayed while at Central Connecticut State University.

My sister and I have never been closer, and I can honestly say she is my best friend.

My friend Mackenzie has been there for me through all the hard times, and she and her boyfriend, Filipe, have been responsible for keeping my spirits up this past year when I was disappointed by not being able to attend Wellesley.

My boyfriend, Max, has been amazing, and just being with him inspires me to be a better person.

Additionally, the friends who colluded with me at the casino have been cut out of my life completely, and their leader, Cole Porter, is currently awaiting trial.

Over this year, I've done my best to learn from my parents' example of integrity and determination (my father, who was laid off last year, recently landed a job at a smaller company, for less money, but is hopeful he will work his way up as the economy gets stronger, and my mother has recently returned to work full-time after a months-long job search so that my sister and I can attend the schools of our choice), and I've realized that there are no shortcuts when it comes to achieving the things you want.

And while I'm certainly enjoying my experience here at Central Connecticut State, I am confident that Wellesley is the place for me to really grow and expand to the best of my academic abilities. I am very familiar with Massachusetts (my boyfriend is currently attending Boston College) and with Wellesley in particular (my friend Parvati is a student and sends me frequent e-mail updates filled with details about what a great school it is).

As you can see, my high school grades are impeccable (except for the slipup those months during my senior year), and I've maintained a

4.0 average here at Central. I've done this while holding a part-time waitressing job to help my parents pay my tuition.

Additionally, my probation ended last year when I turned eighteen, and I have had a clean record ever since.

I am available for an interview at your convenience and very much look forward to hearing back from you.

Sincerely,
Shannon Card

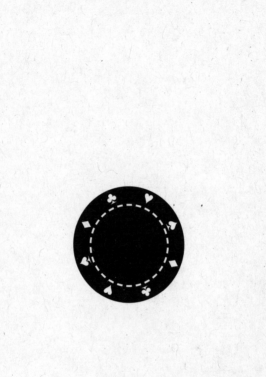